First paperback edition November 2018

For information regarding special discounts on bulk orders or for teachers, schools and librarians, address Richard Holeman Writes 3648 Raven Drive Lake Elsinore, CA 92530

Contact the author via email at
rh@richardholemanwrites.com

richardholemanwrites.com
Facebook.com/RichardHolemanWrites

Discover Richard Holeman on goodreads.com

<u>By Richard Holeman</u>
First Boy on the Moon
Never Ring a Witch's Doorbell
Haloes are for Show-Offs

SOUTHERN HIGHWAY GOSPEL COMPANION

A STORY BY RICHARD HOLEMAN

This one is for Kathy

I still like the way you pray

Acknowledgements

As always, thank you for helping me
pick out my assorted screw-ups.

Kathryn Davis
Stephen Leigh
Debbie Martin
Jennifer Hanners

Like a bird that wanders from her nest, so is a man who wanders from his home.

- Proverbs 27:8

...for God has heard the voice of the boy from the place where he is.

- Genesis 21:17

And there will be a highway...

- Isaiah 11:16

COTTONMOUTH BLUES

If you come along
Walking with me
You better put on
Your traveling shoes
You've got to learn
To love the blues
To be the bearer
Of bad news
And don't bring anything
With you
That you can't afford to lose
Better hurry and
Better pack light
If we sleep in the day
We'll move faster by night
Where the devil can't smell us
And we're out of God's sight
If you're following me
I've gone south
Down a highway, deadly
Like a cottonmouth

PART ONE

THE KING'S HIGHWAY

ONE
SOUTHBOUND AND DOWN

By the time the wind blew me down through Dixie, I had been on the road four years, but never tripped through the south. When I lit out of Jersey in '82, I followed the northern routes on my way to California and once I went west, I was lost. I spent years chasing the seasons up and down the Pacific coast and wandering the big empty of the southwestern deserts. In the spring of 1986, I finally backtracked east as far as Ohio, then detoured south.

It was a memory of my mother that sent me south out of Ohio and into Kentucky. I was sitting in a truck stop diner in the middle of a rainy night, nursing a fifty-four-cent cup of coffee and smoking too many cigarettes, when *that* old ghost came to call.

The DRIVERS ONLY section of the café had all the amenities that most of the bigger truck stops afforded their preferred customers. The truckers got better and faster service than everybody else and the waitress in that section was funny and flirty instead of sarcastic and grumpy. There were telephones mounted on the counter so the drivers could check in with their wives or their freight company and, if one of them didn't have anybody to call in the middle of the night, he could pop a quarter in the table-top jukebox and play his favorite songs without getting up from his biscuits and gravy.

I knew the rules about sitting at the DRIVERS ONLY counter. If I was with a trucker who had invited me in off the road for a meal, I'd sit with him and the waitress wouldn't even look sideways at me, but if I was alone, they knew right away I was a hitchhiker, even though I always stashed my pack outside. It was almost as if they could smell the low road on me.

That night, I was taking up space in a corner booth of the smoking section, but I was listening to the truckers' idle talk across the room. In their jokes about the road, rants about the highway patrol and moans over the price of diesel and coffee, there were hints about their destinations and their demeanors. Sometimes I could tell which drivers were more likely to give me a ride just by the things that they said or how much they did or didn't laugh.

I heard one of the truckers complain that it was too quiet in the diner and he plunked a quarter in the jukebox, made his selections and sent me down a black velvet hole into the past.

Elvis Presley, nearly ten years in his grave and *still* the King of Rock and Roll, filled the café with his beautiful, otherworldly voice. He sang 'Love Me Tender' from beyond the veils of time and death and I closed my eyes, dragged deeply on my cigarette and recalled a night when I was ten years old and Elvis and my mother were still alive.

I had snuck out of the apartment and across town to the cemetery where we had buried my grandmother that summer. Mom had caught me coming home in the middle of the night and I had expected a beating for staying out so late, but instead of punishing me, she had played that record, her favorite Elvis Presley song, and we danced in the dark until I fell asleep on my feet.

That memory of my mother was the one I carried closest to my heart and since she died, it had become something more than just a fond recollection. It was such a fine memory, hidden away so long among others deadlier and darker, that it faded and folded with time until it was a painful sort of myth. I buried it deeper still, low down in my soul, in that open wound where I had built a shrine to all the ghosts that haunted my heart.

The waitress pulled me back from the past and almost caught me crying, appearing silently on crepe-soled shoes to top off my lukewarm coffee with a tilt of a steaming pot. She noticed my scant tears and met them with an awkward frown.

"Listen, kiddo," she said, low enough not to embarrass me in front of the other customers, "That's your last refill for the night. Fifty-four cents is pretty cheap rent for the last four hours."

I looked around the diner. It was mostly empty at three o'clock in the morning, except for the trucker's counter, which was bound to be full any time of day or night. She didn't need the booth and I had money to buy another round of coffee if I really wanted to stay, but I knew she wanted me to move along and, outside, the rain had weakened to an ambitious mist.

I handed her a dollar bill and left the refill steaming on the table.

The truck stop lot was bright beneath harsh, buzzing lamps, but I crossed into the shadows along the fence and found the tall brush where I had stashed my gear. I thought about hanging around and talking up some of the drivers as they climbed back into their rigs, but the lot was quiet, full as it was with eighteen-wheelers. All of the drivers were inside the truck stop, eating in the café or showering upstairs, or shut up in the sleepers of their trucks.

There was a thin stand of trees at the back end of the lot and I considered making camp. The rain was light enough now that I could set up my tent without getting drenched, but I was too wired after four hours of slurping thick, black coffee to go to sleep. Anyway, I'd be better off if I made camp down the road apiece, out in the woods, instead of fifty yards off the back door of the truck stop office.

I heaved my worn canvas duffle over the chain-link fence and climbed up after it. I landed hard on the soggy ground and slipped on my ass, soaking and soiling my clothes with slick Ohio mud. I took the risk of changing my clothes right there in the tall brush along the interstate and strapped my knife to my belt, in reach and out of sight beneath a long flannel shirt.

I wanted music, something to chase the echoes of 'Love Me Tender' out of my ears, but the weather was too wet to risk my Walkman or any of my cassette tapes so I left them buried deep in my pack, safe and dry in plastic bags. I left the truck stop behind and walked up to the highway with the ghosts of Elvis Presley and my mother dancing together in my mind. In that moment, I decided where I would go when I left Ohio behind me and I crossed beneath an overpass and settled in on the southbound ramp.

Traffic was thin, but I knew it would pick up once the truckers sleeping over in the lot at the *Flying J* woke up and got their big wheels back out on the road. I sat on my duffel bag, leaned back against a signpost and pulled my harmonica from the folds of my leather jacket. I tried a little roadside blues and I faked a couple Springsteen riffs, but I settled absentmindedly into a sad and lonesome slide that I recognized as the melody of 'Love Me Tender.'

Before the sun came up, when the eastern edge of the sky began to break the faintest pink behind grey clouds, the truckers woke up and the storm did, too. Big trucks, bobtail or hauling trailers, chugged beneath the overpass and swung past me, grunting through the low gears, on their way up the steep ramp and down the interstate. The rain was falling hard and warm and I stood back from the edge of the road, where the soft shoulder was going quickly to mud, and stuck my thumb out like a beggar pointing south.

I was wet enough to be grouchy, but I didn't expect to wait too long on a ride. The early morning rush out of the truck stop only stacked the odds in my favor that one of the truckers would be the kind to give a kid a lift and the long, slow haul up the grade gave them a chance to take a good, long look before they made up their mind about me. I was drenched, but I was clean. I needed a shave, but my hair was neat and I knew damned well that the rain falling hard on my face made me look younger and more vulnerable than I really was.

It's only human nature, I suppose, that we're more sympathetic when it rains and before the day was fully broken, a big cherry-red Peterbilt, dragging a flatbed stacked with iron pipes, flashed its lights and slowed to a crawl so I could climb up on the step-side on the fly. The truck was already picking up speed when I yanked the door open wide enough to scramble inside the tractor and pull my heavy pack in behind me.

I slammed the door against the storm, stuffed my bag on the floorboard and wiped the rain out of my eyes. There was a plastic bobble-head Jesus on the dashboard of the truck and on the radio, a preacher was screaming at the top of his lungs about the quiet peace of God's everlasting arms. I looked across the cab at the driver, a big, bearded bear of a man in a work shirt and coveralls, holding his hand out in expectation of my own.

"Whoooweeee, ain't you just about soaked straight through!" he shouted over the radio preacher's sermon, pumping my hand up and down with his, "If you got some dry clothes, go on back in the sleeper and get into 'em."

I did just that, drawing the curtain closed behind me in case he was the kind to cop a look, and when I came out fresh and dry and settled into the passenger seat, he turned the radio down and introduced himself.

"Dalton Cummings," he said, "Born and raised in Alabama all my life, bound for Nashville with a load o' pipe."

I worked my hand out of his enthusiastic grip and told him my name, but didn't mention where I'd been born and raised. He took a guess at it anyway.

"You're a Yankee, that's for sure. You ain't a New York boy, are you?"

He said "New York boy" with a drawn-out slur, as if it were a curse he shouldn't speak, so I assured him that I was just a kid straight out of Jersey and he settled both hands on the big steering wheel and grinned.

"Well, I can get you all the way through Kentucky and on into Nashville so's long as you don't mind listenin' to the Word of The Lord." He reached out and turned a knob on the radio, assaulting my ears and my soul with the rantings and ravings of *Reverend Johnson Beal's Old Time Radio Revival Hour.*

Dalton Cummings didn't talk over the preaching and I dozed with my eyes wide open while Reverend Beal screamed and panted about the wicked worldliness of rock and roll music and how the devil used that dirty beat to turn America's teenagers into sex-starved sinners. On the dashboard, Jesus nodded his bobble-head up and down and shook it from side to side, agreeing or disagreeing with the good reverend, not by divine wisdom, but the whims of the bumps in the road we travelled over.

"That's all you get comin' over the airwaves these days, friends: the seductive song of Satan and the throbbing pulse of *sex*!" His voice was high and nasal and he sounded over-excited and cheap, like a used car salesman or a late-night-television-mattress-king. "Twenty-four hours a day, friends! Seven days a week, brothers and sisters! It's sin set to music and they beam it right into *your* fine Christian homes, into the very rooms where your children sleep! Don't even get me started on that stinkin' MTV! Friends, that's just the same ol' whore in a brand-new dress!"

The studio audience erupted in rapturous support of Reverend Beal, but he shushed them with his fire and brimstone shouts. He hollered that the only rock and roll that mattered to God was the rock rolled away from Jesus' tomb.

"America's children need John the Baptist, not John Lennon!"

I thought the reverend was about seven years late in condemning the murdered Beatle, but I kept my mouth shut.

"Your kids are gettin' loaded on marijuana and magic dragons when the real Peter, Paul and Mary are alive and well in the pages of the New Testament!"

His voice was reaching a trembling, fevered pitch and he sounded truly anguished when he spit out the proof that his carnal knowledge of rock and roll sin wasn't as behind the times as it sounded.

"THE WORLD NEEDS GOD AND MOSES, NOT GUNS 'N' ROSES!"

The faithful studio audience of the *Old Time Radio Revival Hour* clapped their hands, shouted amen and hallelujahs and faded into a commercial promising speedy delivery of an actual sliver of wood recovered from the remains of Noah's Ark; only nineteen-ninety-five, plus shipping and handling, of course.

Dalton Cummings lowered the radio volume and glanced at me across the cab. "Reverend Beal, he's the real deal, son," he said around a true believer's smile, "I always listen to him when I'm out on the road. When I can't get preachin' on the radio, I got the whole Bible on cassette tape. The old *and* new testaments."

I nodded and so did bobble-head Jesus, and Dalton Cummings continued to testify.

"Yep, I keep the Word close out here on the road and it's a right blessing listenin' to them Bible tapes, but that Reverend Beal is the *deal*. That's what I always say."

Well, I didn't know whether or not that was something he *always* said, but he'd told me twice in two minutes and I held my tongue instead of asking him why he thought a man preaching the Bible on the radio was the real deal, rather than the book itself. Dalton Cummings had offered to take me all the way to Nashville. That was a good, long haul and I didn't want to risk insulting his Christian sensibilities and being put out in the rain.

I hoped that Dalton would tire of his own voice and let the radio do the preaching again, so I could catch a little sleep. The trucker expected at least the appearance that I was paying attention to the conversation, but the preachers on the radio couldn't look sideways at me if I nodded off against the window while they wailed. Two hours into a six-hour drive, Dalton Cummings was still witnessing and I wondered if he might shut up if I stopped hoping and started praying.

"A fella's gotta be extra mindful of sin out here on the road," he said. He nodded his head up and down and I stole a glance at bobble-head Jesus to see if he agreed, but he had spun his head halfway around to stare out the windshield at the rain and road.

"Yep, yep...when a man leaves his wife and his home and gets out truckin' down the road, best thing *he* can do is keep his eyes on heaven."

I thought of a joke and I told it.

"Wouldn't he be better off if he kept at least one of his eyes on the road?"

Dalton Cummings didn't laugh or even chuckle, but his expression was earnest rather than annoyed.

"Son, that's just me speakin' figuratively," he said, "But I guess the truth is, if you keep both eyes on The Lord, He'll watch the road for you."

Just then, a feathery flash of brown and white burst into the glow of the truck's headlights and startled us both, but The Lord must have seen the hawk because instead of dying against the windshield, it flapped its great wings and escaped with a shriek over the top of the cab and into the rainy sky.

"Whoooweeee, boy!" Dalton Cummings shouted, "You see that? That's God right there, keepin' us from harm!"

I nodded my head and so did the dashboard Jesus, but it seemed to me that it was the hawk, not the two of us, God had been keeping from harm.

Dalton Cummings took a long draw from a thermos and said, "Now, where was I before we got interrupted by the hand of God?"

I don't know why I did it, but I reminded him.

"You were talkin' about how a trucker's gotta be extra mindful of sin."

"That's right," he said, "But not just truckers, kid. That's good advice for anybody out on the road, right on down to hitchhikin' tramps."

Dalton Cummings might have known where sin lay waiting for long-haul truckers, but I had been a long time on the road and I knew it was different for hitchhiking tramps. Oh, I'd met the devil out on the highway a time or two, sure, but it seemed to me he mostly set up shop closer to the towns, where business was steady, not just passing through.

"On the road, a fella's lost even when he knows where he's headed," Dalton said, "You got all kinds of temptations along the highway, amen. You got casinos and smut shops and when you roll into the truck stop for the night, ain't the lots just full of weak women lookin' to lead you straight astray?"

Something in the way his certainty wandered into a question made me suspicious that Dalton Cummings, God-fearing, truck-driving evangelist, had fallen prey to those truck stop Jezebels a time or two himself. I couldn't know and I wouldn't dare to ask him about *that*, but something I felt sure of all on my own was that the women who worked the lots were usually the ones who had been led astray, turned out by one kind of man to give cheap, rented satisfaction to another kind.

If Dalton Cummings didn't see it that way, who was I to fault him? He was only doing what men had been doing since the opening chapters of the Book of Genesis; when it comes to carnal sin, blame the woman God made.

On the radio, by coincidence or a divine sense of ironic humor, the *Old Time Radio Revival* and its frothing host were followed by a soft-spoken woman reading gently from the Bible and Dalton Cummings reached for the dashboard and clicked the radio into silence.

"I don't hold with women preachers," he huffed, "Says right in the Bible 'let your women keep silence in the churches.' I ain't one to be preached at by a woman; no sir. Besides, that one on the radio...she's got the short hair like a man."

On the dash, the plastic Jesus rocked his head back and forth, but I don't think he was agreeing with the trucker so much as showing off his beautiful long brown hair.

In the absence of the radio, I expected Dalton to pop in one of his cassette recordings of The Bible, but he seemed more interested in conversation than conversion, at least for the moment.

"You're a long ol' ways from home, boy." He took another pull of coffee from his thermos and said, "What you doin' down south, anyway?"

I pushed my hair back from my forehead, curled up the corner of my lip and did my best Elvis Presley. "Ah'm a-goin' to Graceland."

"Graceland!" Dalton Cummings looked at me like I'd told him I was on my way to a brothel or a Bible burning. "Boy, didn't you even hear a blamed thing Reverend Beal was preachin' about?"

"Sure, I heard him," I said. I wanted to remind Dalton that the radio had been turned up so loud all of northern Kentucky probably heard the sermon, but instead I said, "I just don't hear the sin he was hollerin' about."

Dalton Cummings' mouth stretched into a disapproving frown and he scowled at me across the cab.

"Son, that ol' devil turns you deaf to the Word," he said, "Believe me you, those rock and roll singers are goin' straight to hell and Elvis is already there waitin' on 'em. He might just be the worst of 'em all!"

The truck hit a bump in the road and bobble-head Jesus, obviously an Elvis fan, got all shook up.

"The worst of 'em all," Dalton Cummings repeated softly.

I shook my head in disagreement and resigned myself to the idea that my ride across Kentucky was growing shorter by the moment.

"Well, what about all those gospel records Elvis made?"

Dalton shook his head. "Shoot! That hillbilly singin' gospel music is an insult to Jesus and to any true Christian. You can't sing praises to The Lord while you're callin' yourself The King!"

He scowled out the windshield at the road and the quieting rain. "Idolatry," he said softly, "Besides...he sings like a nigger."

His fingers hovered over the radio's volume knob, but instead of turning up the preaching he said, "Ain't you a little young to be an Elvis Presley fan?"

I shrugged my shoulders.

"I don't know," I said, "I go more for Springsteen, but my mom loved Elvis. I'm goin' to Graceland for her. She would've went one day if she'd lived."

Dalton Cummings sighed and faked a smile.

"Well, I'm sorry your momma passed," he said, "But I gotta tell you, kid, she taught you all wrong about that rock and roll music."

I leaned across the cab and felt my lip curl up again, but this time it felt more like a mean dog's snarl than a bad Elvis impression.

"Say another word about my mother and I'll reach across there and smack your stupid face."

His eyes went wide and his face went red, as if I'd already slapped him and he worked the brake and the clutch and slowed the big Peterbilt until it rolled to a stop on the shoulder of the highway.

"You get the hell outta my truck," he hissed, "Get the hell out and take the devil with you."

I pushed open the door with one hand, grabbed my pack with the other and climbed out onto the sidestep, but before I jumped down to the blacktop, I looked back into the cab at Dalton Cummings.

"Hey," I said, "Isn't God everywhere? Ain't He out here on the road, too?"

Dalton smirked at me and said, "You better believe He is, boy. He's everywhere we go."

I smirked back. "Well, shit," I said, "Why you so afraid of the devil, then?"

I stood on the shoulder of the road, somewhere in Kentucky, with the rain falling softly all around me and watched the truck roll away down the highway. There were two stickers slapped on the rear end of the trailer. One read I BRAKE FOR ANGELS and the other said THIS VEHICLE MAKES FREQUENT STOPS.

TWO
GOD SPELLED BACKWARDS

I had blown my ride, but I was glad to be out of Dalton Cumming's rig and back out on the road, where God was a little more soft-spoken. It was only mid-morning and traffic along the highway was steady, but I hadn't slept in almost two days and the caffeine that had kept me awake and shaky had worn off.

The storm had blown over thin and the rain was just a damp annoyance I could sleep through. I hauled my pack over a wobbly barbed wire fence into the woods and, forty yards from the highway, I made camp beneath the dripping branches of dogwoods and sugar maple trees.

It wasn't cold enough to need a fire, but all I had for food was a tin of Spam so I scrounged around in the brush for fallen branches that weren't too wet to burn. You can eat Spam straight out of the can, but it's really only any good when it's seared crisp and charred around the edges so I built a small smoky fire, cut the Spam into thick strips, skewered them on thin, wet sticks and set them directly over the low flames to cook.

I had two books in my duffel bag, both of them gifted to me by a man who'd given me a ride across Wyoming a year earlier. I'd read both books several times and I preferred Steinbeck to Twain, but I considered my location, dug past *East of Eden* and pulled *Adventures of Huckleberry Finn* from my pack. I lit a cigarette and settled down to read beneath the flap of my tent while the Spam sizzled and popped over the fire.

I was familiar enough with the story that I could open the book to any page and pick up Huck's trail down to the Mississippi and I read a chapter, pausing every so often to turn the roasting Spam until it was charred crisp all over and ready to eat. I put the book away to keep grease off the pages and I ate the meat hot and steaming from the sticks. I had finished two sizzled strips and was about to start on a third when I heard a stirring in the brush and leaned out of the tent to have a look around.

I had expected a cop, come to tell me to douse my fire and move along, or another tramp, come to beg some of my meat, and my second guess turned out to be a pretty good one. Instead of a greasy hobo, though, a thin and smiling brown dog crept out from the shadows of the trees, sat beside the fire and stared across the flames at my meal.

I knew a stray when I saw one. Hell, I *was* a stray. He didn't look like a bad dog, just down on his luck, and I plucked the strip of Spam from the end of the stick and tossed it across the fire. He caught it in his mouth and looked so proud about it that as soon as he'd gobbled it down, I tossed him the last strip of meat as a reward. He still looked hungry, but so was I and he seemed to take my word for it when I told him we'd eaten all I had. I thought he would slip off into the woods again, back the way he'd come, but he apparently wasn't the kind to eat and run, because he settled down in the damp dust beside the fire and slept. His snoring reminded me that I was tired, too, and I settled into my bedroll and fell asleep to the sound of leftover rain falling from the trees and traffic spraying past out on the highway.

I woke up in the early afternoon and the dog was curled up at my feet in the open end of the tent. The clouds had blown away and the sun was out and steaming up the woods and I tried to shoo the dog off into good weather, but he stayed around while I broke camp and followed me up to the highway, even though I hollered at him that I traveled alone and didn't have any more Spam.

I sat on my duffel, leaned back against a signpost and spent the next two hours arguing with the dog. I reasoned, but he cocked one ear and ignored me with the other. I persuaded, but he wouldn't be persuaded. I threatened him and cursed gruffly at him, but he knew that I was harmless and he settled in the dirt at my feet and slept again, as if he didn't even care that no one was going to pick me up if they thought I was traveling with a damp and mangy mutt.

Twice, I tried to ditch out on the dog while he dozed, but he was a light sleeper and both times he caught me and held me hostage with his lonesome stare.

The first time, I slung my pack silently and meant to sneak up the ramp and out of sight, but the moment my boots crunched in the dirt, this mutt that hadn't wiggled a whisker at the sounds of the traffic passing by, raised his head and wagged his tail and stood up to follow me. Of course, he was happy to stay as long as I did and the moment I sat down again, he lay his chin softly on his paws and settled into snoring.

I waited almost an hour before I made my second attempt at escape and that time I took off my boots and tip-toed slowly down the shoulder toward the woods. I didn't make a sound. I didn't snap a twig or bend a branch, but before I made it to the fence and freedom, I heard a gruff bark and turned around. The fool whose heart I'd won with two strips of flame-cooked Spam was sitting at the top of the embankment, wagging his tail and leaning forward, smiling at the thought of tagging along wherever it was I'd decided to go in just my socks.

Outsmarted by a dog, I returned to the on-ramp and the signpost and decided I'd been going about things all wrong. If he wasn't going to let me leave, I'd make *him* want to leave. I waited until he was comfortably back in his nap and slipped my harmonica out of my jacket. I wrapped my lips around the harp and I honked on the low end and blew shrill shrieks out the high end. The dog woke with a start, raised his head and shook his snout. His ears perked up and twisted and I thought he'd bolt and run, but he just gave me a slow, sly glance, threw his head back and howled along.

I was standing with my hands in the air, arguing with the dog again, when a little Japanese pickup truck crunched to a stop on the edge of the road and a woman honked the horn and hollered at me.

"Come on if you want a ride," she said, "Get your dog up in the back and you can ride up here with me."

THREE
LUANNA

I leaned into the open passenger-side window and told her the dog wasn't mine, that he'd just been tagging along at my heels all day long, but the dog stood on his hind legs and leaned into the window, too, and told her with his grin that I was lying.

She leaned across the cab, reached out and scratched the dog behind his floppy ears. I noticed the deep dive of her white cotton blouse, the generous curve of her breasts, but I was embarrassed and I dragged my eyes back up to her face.

"He's not yours?" she said, "He sure seems to think *you're* his."

I hitched my pack up higher on my shoulder and shook my head.

"He's just a stray," I told her, "He found me in the woods and hasn't left me alone since."

She laughed and said, "Don't take offense, honey, but you look a bit of a stray yourself. Your dog or not, we can't leave him on the side of the road. He's bound to get hit by a truck, if we do."

The dog put his cool snout to my face and slobbered his tongue up my cheek, but I pushed his love away and sighed. "I can't take a dog down the road with me," I said, "What am I gonna do with him?"

The woman looked me over with a suspicious sidelong glance.

"You feed this dog?" she asked me and I'm certain that the truth was in my face. "You *did*! You *fed* him, didn't you?"

"Yeah..." I confessed, "But nothing good. I gave him Spam."

She laughed.

"Fool, you know you can't feed a stray dog and expect him to go back to bein' alone and hungry. You want a ride, you get that dog up in the back and climb on in."

I sighed and asked her the same question I had just a moment ago. "But what am I gonna do with a dog out on the road?"

"We can figure that out while we drive."

I went around to the rear bumper, dropped the tailgate, tossed my duffel into the bed of the truck and the dog leapt in right after it. Why wouldn't he? He had known all along that he'd be going for a ride.

Up in the cramped cab, I settled back on the passenger side, my knees pressed uncomfortably against the glove compartment and noticed an open pack of Kools on the dash.

"Smoke in here?" I asked, reaching into my pocket for my own cigarettes.

"Smoke 'em if you got 'em, honey" she laughed, reaching for the Kools. She shook one from the pack, slipped it between full lips and slipped me a sideways grin. "What's your name, blue eyes?"

I blew smoke out the open window and told her.

"You ain't a natural-born Rick, though. I can tell. You look like a Richard."

I'm sure I must have frowned and when I spoke, there was a bitterness on the tip of my tongue. "I don't go by Richard," I said, "Not ever anymore."

She glanced over at me. "No? Why not?"

"That's my father's name," I told her, "I hate him."

She drew a sharp breath and shook her head. "Now, that's a hard thing for a boy to say 'bout his daddy. What you got against him so bad you gotta hate him over it?"

I hated him for walking out when I was two years old and never coming back. I hated him for giving me the same cold blue eyes he had, but never coming around to look in them. I hated him for finally calling on the telephone, years too late, on the day my mother died, but mostly I hated him for not being man enough to call back after I hung up on him in grief and anger.

I didn't know why I had told her anything at all about my father or how I felt about him. Most of the time I never even thought of him, but whenever anyone called me by my birth name, the name I'd inherited from him right along with my blue eyes and unruly hair, I was reminded of him. *That* was my reason for changing my name to Rick when I had outgrown the boy everyone used to call Richie.

"Everything," I said, "I've got everything against him."

We drove on a few miles in silence, both of us smoking again, and I could tell the quiet was making her uncomfortable by the way she started to softly hum. I couldn't name the song she hummed, but it was vaguely familiar and I was sure it was an old spiritual I'd heard a time or two before.

"You never told me your name..." I offered.

She turned to tell me and for only a moment, I fell in love with her slight smile.

"Luanna," she said, "You say it *that* way; like it sounds. *Loo-wanna*. I'll tell you somethin' about that dog of yours."

I glanced at her across the cab. "He's not my dog. He really is just a stray."

"Whether he is or he isn't," she said, "That dog's the only reason I pulled over to give you a ride."

I laughed, but Luanna scowled at me from behind the steering wheel.

"You laugh like I'm joking," she said, "That's a handsome dog. You...honey, you're about as scruffy lookin' as a badger on a bender."

Driving south on 65, we were good company and the dog was happy in the back, hanging his head over the bed of the pickup and lapping up the passing highway breezes. The last straggling storm clouds had thinned to veils of lace against blue sky and we rode with the windows down, smoking and talking and listening to Marvin Gaye on the dashboard cassette player. The stereo in Luanna's little import truck wasn't much, just a stock system, but music that great sounds good on anything and Luanna turned the volume up loud when she noticed that I was getting into it.

"You know Marvin Gaye?"

"Not really," I told her, "Just from the radio."

We rode along and grooved and I decided that Marvin Gaye knew a lot more about God and men than that preacher on the radio in Dalton Cummings' Peterbilt; Reverend Johnson Beal. I also thought bobble-head Jesus would have been much happier here on Luanna's dashboard, bobbing along to *What's Goin' On* instead of all that old-time gospel radio bullshit.

We didn't talk much while the music played. We drove into the late afternoon, smoking cigarettes, and I stole quick glances at Luanna when I thought that I felt sly and she wouldn't notice. She was older than me, a dozen years older at least, but I thought that she was beautiful.

She had dark curls that fell softly just above dark eyes and her mouth formed the full red shape of a heart when she smiled. Her legs stretched out long and beige below the faded fringe of cutoff jeans and she drove barefoot. Her toes were painted purple at the tips.

We passed through small towns and when we got to Bowling Green, Luanna traded the interstate for a rural highway where the houses thinned out and the woods grew thick along the roadside. We had listened through *What's Goin' On* twice and Luanna popped the cassette out of the player and swapped it for a Doobie Brothers tape.

At a lonesome filling station, I pumped the gas and let the dog drink from a water hose while Luanna went inside to pay and came out with two bottles of Pepsi. Pulling out of the lot, back onto the blacktop, Luanna turned to me and smiled.

"I shouldn't have asked about your daddy back there," she said, "It isn't any business for a stranger."

I smiled back and shook my head.

"Nothin' to be sorry for," I told her, "*I* brought him up."

She left it at that, and I did, too. The Doobie Brothers rocked us down the highway and our talk turned lighter as the afternoon stretched longer and began to yawn. She told me she worked in a department store, dressing mannequins for display, but that she was also an artist. She was on her way now to finish a landscape she'd been painting for weeks.

"I paint so slow," she sighed.

The sun was rushing west beyond the woods, the dog was asleep in the back and Luanna pulled the little truck off the highway and onto the shoulder.

She shifted into neutral and let the truck idle with her bare foot pressing on the brake pedal.

"I'm gettin' off the highway here," she said, "I don't suppose it's a very good spot to catch a ride."

I hadn't seen many other cars on the highway since we'd left the interstate back at Bowling Green, there wasn't a market or a gas station in sight and the intersection we were parked at didn't have so much as a flashing yellow light. Still, I had been let off in worse places and I told her so.

"I can walk it if I have to," I said, "And I'll prob'ly make camp around here before it gets dark."

I looked over my shoulder through the rear window and saw the dog stirring from his sleep now that the ride had ended.

"I've still got *him* to drag around."

She sighed. I wasn't sure what type of a sigh it was.

"Why don't you boys come on with me for now?" she said, "There's a river just down that road. I can drop you back at the interstate when I leave, or there's a nice place in the trees if you camp out."

I shrugged. "I'm not in a hurry to get anywhere."

Luanna put the truck in gear and it lurched down a rough, slender road that wiggled into the yellow and green folds of the forest.

"Where are you goin' anyway?" she said, "You and that handsome dog of yours."

She called me sweet and crazy, going to Graceland to pay my mother's respects to Elvis Presley. I had learned my lesson earlier when I mentioned my father so I kept myself to myself and didn't tell Luanna that my trip to Graceland was more selfish than sweet, though I wouldn't have argued the crazy part.

When I left Jersey, I thought that I would be leaving my mother's ghost behind, but in the years since then I had dragged her with me down the road and she had haunted me wherever I wandered. I couldn't lose her because I couldn't lose myself. When she died, we had been fighting, furiously and frequently. We spoke hateful vows to one another and she had become ill and passed away before we could take them back.

I thought that by going to Graceland, to the place where her King had lived and died, I could finally do something that *pleased* her. Maybe she would stay there, haunting the Jungle Room, and let me go my way alone.

"Hey...you hear what I said?"

Luanna's voice pulled me out of myself and I blinked at her. The truck was parked beneath the cape of a low willow tree, on the banks of a slow river, and Luanna was standing on the driver's side, leaning into the cab with her hand on the back of the seat.

"Scooch out and get your dog," she said, "So I can get behind the seat."

The dog was out of the truck and bounding through the brush down to the water. I got out and hollered at him, but he wasn't coming back until he was ready so I left him to splash in the shallows and I dragged my duffel bag over the tailgate and onto my shoulder.

Luanna had pulled a folding easel from behind the pickup's seat and set it up on a mossy mound where the bank slouched down to the river. She went back to the truck once more for her canvas and paints and while she filled her pallet and chose her brush, I looked past the easel and saw the same wooden bridge with big brass fixtures, red against shimmering blue and whispering green, that I had seen still unfinished on Luanna's canvas.

I left her alone with the bridge and her brush and wandered down to the water. I chased the dog back and forth along the river's edge and sat with him awhile on a patch of damp weeds when we were both tired out and panting.

He was a good dog, but I couldn't drag him along with me all over the countryside. I had no idea what to do about him, but I had to figure out a way to get rid of him.

We were lazy on the green bank of the river, his head in my lap and my fingers scratching his neck, but his ears twitched and mine might have, too, when Luanna called out to us.

"I brought food. You two come up here and get some."

The dog was faster up the slope and faster with his hunk of the big roast beef sandwich and I was still nibbling at mine, stretched out on a big woven blanket Luanna had put out on the grass, while he sat sad-eyed at my feet. If he hadn't been a dog, I would have been sure he was counting every bite I took. I tossed him the last corner of bread and meat and as soon as it was gone, he curled up in the grass for a nap.

FOUR
SOUTHERN COMFORT

Luanna went back to her easel and I rolled a joint and got stoned, listening to the river run and watching her stroke splashes of red, gold and green across the canvas. She painted with her entire body, not just her hand, and I didn't miss the sloping roll of her shoulder as she pushed and pulled the brush or the way she cocked her head, the brush stilled in her hand, and looked out past the canvas at the bridge or the low sunlight on the water. She leaned slightly to her left when she painted and the curve of her hip drew her denim shorts just slightly up her thigh.

A fickle breeze carried the tangy smoke from my joint across the clearing and Luanna turned away from the easel and waggled her brush at me. Drops of red fell from the bristles and colored the leaves at her feet.

She put down her brush and palette, crossed the clearing to sit beside me and the dog hardly stirred between us. I offered her the joint, she took it between her fingers and stared at it.

"I haven't smoked in years," she said, "Since college...or just after."

She stared at the joint for another moment and I thought she would hand it back to me, but just as I reached out for it, she put it to her lips and the cherry flared bright orange when she inhaled.

She choked on the smoke, her eyes grew wide and wet and she coughed a great blue cloud. She waved the smoke away from her face and we passed the joint a few more times before she waved that away, too.

"No more," she coughed, "I'm ruined now for painting. That bridge was built in a month and I've been painting it for three."

I stubbed the joint out on my boot and traded it for a cigarette. Luanna lit one of her own and we smoked as the sun sank into its last hour and the buzz of the cheap Mexican weed settled down hard in us both.

She absently stroked the dog's fur and, once or twice, the back of her hand brushed lightly against my shoulder. I pretended not to notice her touch because I was shy and almost sure she hadn't noticed it herself, but when she rolled over on her hip and squeezed the dog out from between us, she pressed her back against my chest and drew my arm across her waist.

I was still shy, but no longer uncertain, and I shifted my body against her thigh and leaned my head so close to hers that my lips nearly brushed the back of her neck.

"Do you catch a lot of rides with women?" she said and for a moment I thought I might boast, but I told her the truth instead.

"Not a lot," I said, "More than I expected when I first hit the road, but not so many that I ever thought much of it."

Her hand was soft on mine and the skin of her belly was silken and smooth.

"I know why they do it," she said softly, "Why they pick you up."

"Well, don't say it's because of the dog," I said, "I've only had *him* since yesterday."

She hooked a foot around my heel and drew our legs into a gentle tangle.

"It's the way you look standin' out on the road," she whispered, "Or maybe not the way you look, but the way you *seem*; wild and young and lost. Dangerous, but vulnerable, too. I think a woman sees a boy like that and she thinks she knows what he needs."

I didn't ask her what I needed, but she told me anyway.

"Some see a boy who needs a mother; some of 'em want to be your sister or your friend."

I was nervous about her touch, but I didn't pull away when her hand guided mine to her breast.

"What kind of boy did you see?" I said.

"The kind who needs all three."

She rolled over and her breath was on my lips, but I hesitated and pulled back from a moment that might have become a kiss.

She smiled her heart-shaped smile and leaned into me.

"Why so shy?" she whispered, "You've never been with a black girl before?"

I leaned back into her.

"Oh, no...I mean, it's not *that*," I said, "I've never been with someone your *age* before."

She looked at me sideways, but before I could take back my accidental insult, she shut me up with the kiss I'd been imagining all afternoon and when I was inside of her, she sighed soft and warm on my mouth.

After, when the breeze came back to the trees and I could hear the river flowing again, she rested briefly in my arms, stoned and rambling.

"That was sweet," she said. I didn't know enough then to make up my mind whether or not it was a compliment.

She moved to get dressed and I pulled on my jeans and took my shirt from the branches of the tree we had lain beneath. She reached into her bag and brought out thirty dollars, but I brushed it away when she tried to stuff it in my palm.

"You need to eat," she said, "And you've got that handsome dog to feed, too."

I took the money and buried it in my pocket.

"I'm not keepin' that dog," I said, "I don't want him."

She grinned and gave me a wink.

"You ought to think twice on that," she said.

"Think twice on what?"

"Chasin' away all the love that God sends you."

She turned back to her truck, stopped to hug the dog, and waved us both goodbye as she drove away through the trees.

Later, I lay on the ground in the cool spring darkness, falling asleep in my bedroll with the dog breathing against my back, the river sneaking by in the night and a breeze murmuring through the leaves like the ghost of her sigh.

FIVE

TO ERR IS HUMAN, TO FORGIVE IS CANINE

Morning came on chilly and when I woke up with the sun, the dog was gone from my side. I couldn't have known if he had left for good during the night or just wandered off, but I didn't waste a moment, in case he was on his way back to my camp. I skipped a fire and coffee, rolled my blankets away in a hurry and pulled on my boots. Sandy sleep still crusted the corners of my eyes and I hadn't even washed my face, but I slung my duffle across my back and hurried through the woods where the crooked river road would lead me back out to the highway.

I felt a little guilty leaving the dog behind, but he had been on his own and getting by before the scent of charred Spam had led him to my fire. He might be lonesome until he forgot me, but the dog would be better off alone on the river than he would be scrounging along the road with *me*. I had enough trouble most of the time just keeping myself fed, let alone safe and dry. Those are the things I told myself, but there was another voice in the back of my mind; Luanna's, reminding me not to chase off the love that God sends my way.

I didn't believe that she had been right about the stray being sent by God, but she was wise to see in me a boy who didn't want to love. Of all the things I had run away from when I lit out down the road, love was the easiest of them all to avoid. Love was scarce on the highway, but it was out there, and when I couldn't outrun it, I chased it away. Sometimes, after it fled, I wanted it back again, but I kept myself safe from my own heart by moving along down the road.

I couldn't see the highway up ahead beyond the trees, but I heard the low rumble of a big truck rattling through and I knew it wasn't far. Ten minutes later, I was standing just off the southbound shoulder with the sun climbing hard in the sky. Passing traffic was thin and I had already made up my mind to walk the highway and put some distance between the dog and myself, but I stopped for a moment in the shade of a hunchbacked tree and let my duffel bag slump to the ground. I dug out my canteen, filled the palm of my hand with water and splashed my face. I dampened my hair, swept it away from my forehead and before I had the cap screwed back on the canteen, a car was slowing along the shoulder.

I hurried with the canteen, got it stowed away in my pack and shouldered the heavy bag. Behind the wheel of the car, an old man tapped on the horn and I hustled toward the roadside and just as I reached to open the passenger door, the early morning quiet was broken by the sound of urgent barking.

I had been found.

The dog came bursting over the slope, his tongue hanging out and flapping, his black eyes wide and excited and his ears flattened with worry. There was a panic in his barking that even I could understand.

Wait for me, wait for me, wait for me.

"That your dog?" the old man said, "I can't have any dog in my car."

He was leaning across the seat, watching the dog hurry toward me and I said, "No, wait. He isn't my dog."

The dog topped the slope, kicking up gravel as he ran along the road's soft shoulder. He bounded in circles around my feet, his tail wagging furiously, and stood on his hind legs with his front paws planted on my chest.

The old man leaned back into the wheel and drove off down the highway and if he had glanced in the rearview mirror as he sped away, he would have seen me fending off kisses from a dog I hardly knew.

I let my duffel slide back to the dirt and stared at the dog. He had calmed himself down to a shaking frenzy and sat at my feet, looking back at me with that panting smile, even though I was sure that he knew I had tried to ditch him.

He licked the back of my hand and hollered at me once.

WOOF!

"Oh, go on and shut up," I said, "God didn't send you *this* time, either."

We walked most of the day along the highway's edge and, even though the traffic had picked up some, no one slowed down to offer us a ride. There were dark clouds gathering far away in the east and the day was turning warm and humid. By late afternoon, I was hungry, grouchy and tired.

I took a rest just off the highway and the dog settled down and stretched out along the length of my duffel bag. I dozed in the shade and was awakened by the sound of car tires crunching on gravel.

"Come on, son, if you're wantin' a lift," a woman called out and a man in the driver's seat waved at me through the windshield.

I slung my pack and started for the sedan with the brown dog at my heels and I heard the woman say, "*Oh*...he's got a *dog*."

The car swung back out on the blacktop and sped away south and I lost my temper with the dog. I turned toward him in a hurry, kicking gravel his way and waving my arms.

"Get away! Go on!" I hollered at him.

His ears flattened out and his smile drew down and I knew he was afraid, but I kept on yelling at him anyway. He backed off a few feet and I turned up the road, but he followed me.

"I said *get*!" I shouted, "Go! Get *outta* here!"

He stood staring at me with his wise black eyes, but the tilt of his head gave away his confusion and when he took another step toward me, I reached down and picked up a stone. It was away, speeding out of my hand before I had even realized what I was doing.

I hadn't meant to hit him. I didn't for a moment think about throwing that rock at the dog. I heaved it hard into the dirt at his paws, meaning to scare him away, to let him know I was serious, but it caught a bounce and hit him hard on his muzzle.

The dog yelped and my heart broke as he turned and ran away from me.

I hadn't noticed it in my angry fit, but there was a car coming fast down the southbound lane. The dog hadn't noticed it, either, and he ran hard out into the lane, directly in front of the car.

I shouted out and the car braked hard, but the dog smacked against the bumper and fell beneath the wheels with a horrible thump that sent him rolling and yelping across the pavement.

No. I didn't mean it.

I ran fast and knelt beside him, cradled him in my arms and cried. He had one good eye, open wide and searching, but the other was sunken, crushed and blind. Beneath his fur, I could feel broken ribs and battered flesh and blood ran from his muzzle.

I heard a car door open behind me and cautious footsteps on the asphalt.

I stared into that single black eye, watching the light fade away from it and the dog dragged his tongue over the back of my hand, sighed a rattling breath and died. I held his still shape against my chest and moaned and cried.

"Oh, Jesus, kid," a voice called over my shoulder, "Was that your dog?"

I turned around and saw a young man in a crisp white shirt standing in the center of the lane, gaping down at me, looking past me at the crumpled body of the dog, horror on his face and in his eyes.

"Yeah," I told him, "He was my dog."

SIX
SHOTGUN FUNERAL

I left a guilty, blood-red footprint on the blacktop and I carried the dog's limp body to the highway's edge. The car that had killed him (*I killed him*) idled on the shoulder of the road, the driver's side door flung open, and the man in the white shirt walked around the Ford's front-end, examining the deadly chrome bumper.

He whistled long and sharp.

"No damage," he drawled, "Whole mess o' blood, though."

I didn't answer and he jammed his hands in the pockets of his slacks and looked at me across the hood of his car. He glanced down at my dead dog and back into my eyes. I wondered if he saw through the blue to my shame. I hoped he had.

"I didn't even see him," he said, "He just run right out in front of me like that. I'm real sorry 'bout your dog, kid."

I shook my head and waved off his apology.

"It's not your fault," I said, "I scared him out onto the road. I shouted at him."

It wasn't a lie, but it was less than a mouthful of the truth and I glanced away from the man's eyes when I told it. My hollering had frightened the dog and put his tail between his legs, but it was the stone that had killed him, as sure as it had been the car. I left the stone out of the story I told the young man because the truth made me feel like a killer instead of a fool. He would have to be satisfied with the shame in my eyes because I couldn't put the whole of it all into words.

"I'm sorry 'bout it just the same," he said, "Get him on off the side o' the road and I'll give you a lift into town. I'd help you an' all, but the blood would mess my shirt. I'm goin' for a job."

I looked over his crisp white shirt and creased black slacks and I felt guilty about the dust on his shiny dress shoes.

"I have to bury him," I said, "I've gotta stay and find a spot to bury him."

He glanced at my duffel bag.

"You even got a shovel?"

I shook my head.

"Hell..." the man said, "How you gonna dig a hole that'll fit him?"

"I don't know. I'll dig it with my hands, if I have to."

I knelt over my duffel to unstrap my bedroll and caught a grey blast from the Ford's exhaust as the car peeled back out onto the highway. I had made the young man an accidental accomplice to my sin and I may have made him late for his job interview in town. I watched the car shrink away and hoped the hiring man didn't pass him over because of the dust on his brand-new shoes.

I peeled a thin grey blanket out of my bedroll and gently wrapped it around the dog, a woolen shroud to hold his body, then his bones. I shouldered my bag, lifted the dead dog to my chest and stole away like a criminal, into the woods, with the sun sneaking west like a witness.

I didn't have to dig the hole by hand, after all. A half-mile or so off the highway, where the woods grew close around a thin, trickling stream, I came across a barbed-wire fence marking someone's property line. I left the dog's carcass on the creekbank, let my duffel bag slip to the ground beside it and climbed a grassy slope to the fence-line.

The ground had been softened by the passing rains and I twisted and yanked a metal fencepole until it broke loose from the earth. I was careful removing the sharp, rusted wire where it was hooked around the pole; still, I cut the back of my hand and tore the sleeve of my shirt on the barbs.

I used the pole as a makeshift pick to break through the soft soil along the stream, but it wasn't much use when it came to removing the loose dirt from the deepening hole. I worked in the fading sunlight, hunched over the pole, digging in the dirt, then down on my knees to empty the hole by hand.

I had been at it nearly a full hour and the grave wasn't deep enough to bury the dog in. I lit a cigarette and rested in the shallow hole, my knees planted in the damp dirt, and I heard a rustling in the woods and a voice call out from behind me.

"Whatcha doin' over there?"

I turned to look and showed both of my hands. A man stood on the slope, just this side of the fence-line, the long grey twin barrels of a shotgun resting across his hip and a boy, wide-eyed and blonde, standing just slightly behind him. The business end of the shotgun was angled toward the ground, but the stock rested easy in the man's big hands and I knew it could strike fast, like a grey metal snake.

"I'm just digging a hole," I said, "It's an accident if I'm on your property."

The man's face was shadowed beneath the wide brim of a hat. I couldn't see his expression, but I could make out his eyes, suspicious but honest, looking me over as he made his way down the slope with the boy following behind him, shaded beneath a wide-brimmed hat of his own.

"Ain't exactly trespassin'," the man said, cocking his head toward the slope, "That's my place back the other side o' the fence."

I nodded, estimated my chance of being shot had just been reduced by at least a third and climbed out of the hole.

"That's *my* fencepole there you're diggin' with, though," the man said, "And you took my wire down some, I guess."

"I did that, yeah. I meant to put it back the way I found it when I'm done digging."

The boy pulled on the man's shirt and said, "But, Daddy...ask him what he's diggin' *for*."

The big man hushed his son, but when he looked back to me, he spoke out the suspicion both of them had. His tone was curious, almost friendly, but the tilt of his gun demanded the truth.

"Does look a might strange," he said, "A fella diggin' out here in the woods alone." He eyed the lump of woolen blanket and drawled, "I'm bound to tell you it looks like you're fixin' to bury a body."

"Sure does," the boy agreed, "Want me to run and tell Ma to get the sheriff?"

I could see the man's face now and he frowned at his son.

"You just stay right here for now and let the man have his say."

I reached out slowly and pulled back a corner of the blanket, showing them the dog's ruined eye and bloodied muzzle. They both nodded.

"Just a dog," I sighed, "He got hit on the highway."

The man leaned his shotgun against the gnarled trunk of a thin tree and the boy leaned in to get a closer look at the dog. He rested his hands on his knees and squinted into the dog's dead eye.

"That's gross," he said.

"Damned shame," the man said, "Your dog?"

I hadn't thought of the brown dog as mine until the moment of his death, but I looked the stranger in his eye and told him the truth.

"He was," I said, "But only for the last couple of days. We were only passing through together."

The man plucked a red and white pack of Winstons from his shirt pocket and lit a cigarette of his own. He drew the smoke in deep, blew it out his nostrils and turned to his son.

"Riley, run and fetch two shovels from out the shed," he said, "And your momma's gonna ask, so you tell her everything's just fine."

"Yes, Daddy; I will."

The boy turned and ran off up the slope, crossed the fallen barbed-wire with a skip and disappeared into the shadows of the trees.

The man's name was Vernon and when his son returned with two shovels and a short length of cedar board, he helped me dig out the hole and after, when I'd rolled the dog gently into the grave, he helped me fill it back in and tamp down the loose dirt. We smoked as the sun descended behind the trees and the boy offered me the cedar slat.

"For markin' the grave," he said, "But I didn't bring anything to write with."

He shrugged.

I had a black permanent marker in my pack; most hitchhikers carried one, for writing out their destination, or just their general direction, on strips of cardboard or for marking messages on the backs of highway signs. I dug the felt-tipped pen out of a flap on my duffel bag and held it poised over the board, deciding what I should write.

"You could just put his name down," the boy offered, "I'll come sometimes and make sure it ain't fallen over."

I didn't tell them that the dog hadn't had a name, but I knew in an instant just what to call him and I printed one word across the cedar board, as neatly as I could over the cracks and knots in the wood, and sunk the plank lengthwise into the earth at the head of the grave.

Dark was falling quickly and we righted the fence together, finishing just as the last light of the day went skimming away west. We smoked, sitting in the dirt at the top of the weedy slope, and he asked me quiet questions, just enough to find out who I was and where I'd come from. I asked him a few questions of my own and learned that the nearest town, Russellville, was a dozen miles south and that I was closer to Tennessee than I had thought.

"Nashville ain't but a couple hours from here," Vernon said, "Mind, it could take two days or more, the way you're travelin' rough."

"I'm not in a hurry," I said.

"Nope," he answered back, "I don't s'pose you are."

He poked a hole in the moist dirt with his finger, stubbed the smoldering butt of his Winston out in the earth and looked at me steady and long.

"You dangerous?" he said, "You a thief or on the run from the law?"

I *was* on the run; I had been for years, but not from any badge, only ghosts and all the memories that I hadn't learned to live down.

"I guess I'm dangerous if I'm in danger," I told him, "But I'm not wanted by the cops or lookin' to get in trouble."

Vernon sighed and got up from the ground, long and lean above me in the twilight. Riley imitated his father's slow rise from the slope and hooked his thumbs through the loops on his jeans.

"C'mon back home with us then," Vernon said, "Get yourself some supper and you can bed down out in the tractor shed."

I thanked him with a handshake and followed them over the fence and across a wide pasture, toward a porchlight shining from a small white house. Cows lulled in the darkness as we passed and when we reached the dooryard, a dog rose from the shadows and barked until he recognized his people. Riley looked up at his father and whistled softly through his teeth.

"Momma's gonna curse you blue, Daddy," he said, "Bringin' home a stranger for supper."

SEVEN
A CLEAN-CUT KID

Vernon's wife *did* curse at him, just a little, but he didn't turn blue and he didn't curse her back. He let her have her say while she looked me up and down from the doorway and once she got over the sight of me, he led me up onto the porch.

"He's a nice enough kid, Carol Ann," Vernon said as we stepped across the threshold of his home, "He ain't out to cause no harm and his dog got killed today."

Carol Ann frowned at her husband, then at me, but most of the hardness lifted from her eyes and she scolded us all with only a little anger in her voice.

"Well, ain't a one of you settin' down to my table as muddy as that," she said. She shooed Riley down the hall to take a bath and sent her husband and I back outside.

"You two clean up at the hose and get outta them dirty jeans an' boots."

The dog, a big hound, followed us to the back of the house where we washed up in cold well water, splashing fresh mud on our boots and jeans, but coming away with clean faces and hands.

Vernon led me out to the tractor shed and showed me where I could roll out my blankets, in a dark back corner of the bare dirt floor where a stack of dusty pads and tarps were stacked against the knotted wall.

"Come on up to the house once you're changed," he said, "Carol Ann won't hold her temper as long as she'll hold supper."

I put on fresh clothes and rinsed my muddy ones in a basin and hung them across the tractor's wide plow to dry. I smoked a cigarette on my way back up to the house and when Carol Ann answered my knock at the door, I left my boots out on the porch and followed her to her table.

There was a prayer and then fried chicken so good it made me wonder how I could not believe in God, but still feel blessed. We passed bowls of mashed potatoes and peas and Vernon told me proudly that the milk on the table had come from his own cows. His wife was mostly quiet and she wasn't very good at pretending she was glad to have me in her home for supper, but she smiled politely when I thanked her and told her how good her cooking was.

Over warm apple pie, Vernon told me about his cows and the farm he had inherited from his father.

"I've been workin' these fields since I could walk 'em," he said, "I'll work 'em 'til I'm gone and dead and my boy, he'll do the same."

He was boasting, and he had a right to, but the particular circle of life he took such pride in seemed to me to be a broken wheel. I didn't speak it out but I wondered if it was the men who worked the land or did the earth work *them*, bending one generation until it broke and passed its yoke down to the next?

I wasn't anyone to judge a life, though. I had chosen a life that wasn't one at all and when our talk turned to my travels, it was Riley who had most of the questions.

"You just go around and get in any ol' car with strangers?"

I suppose it was like that in the beginning when I was green, but I had learned to tell a lot from a person's eyes or their tone of voice and there had been car doors I didn't open and rides I didn't take. I trusted those instincts when I felt them, but I was still a kid, really, and intuition wasn't always enough to keep me safe from harm, or from the threat of it.

Riley pushed his dessert plate, empty of even a crumb, to the center of the table, sat back in his chair and stared at me with wide eyes. He was young, maybe eleven, but certainly not yet twelve, and I could see in his expression that a life like mine frightened him, but not nearly as much as it intrigued him.

"You're like a hobo," he said, "Do you ever work?"

Hobo seemed like an old-fashion word and I told him that I mostly called myself a tramp, when I had to call myself anything at all. I worked when I could find it, sometimes for an hour or a day lumping freight for truckers and other times, I settled down for weeks and even months if there was a job at a truck stop or a diner. Once, I had spent an entire winter on an apple orchard in Washington State and another year, I went from town to town with a traveling carnival.

Riley leaned forward with another question in his eyes, but his mother interrupted him. Carol Ann gave me a look that warned me not to fill her boy's head with romantic notions of my highway life and pushed her own pie plate away from her.

"That seems like a lonesome, dirty way for a boy to live," she said, "Just how old are you, anyway?"

"I'm twenty, ma'am. Since January."

Carol Ann frowned and folded her napkin neatly on the table in front of her.

"Twenty years old," she said, "Still a boy and likely bound to stay one as long as you keep on living this way, without a family or even Jesus"

Vernon glanced at me uncomfortably and I shifted in my chair, but I spared him from intervening by agreeing with his wife.

"Yes, ma'am," I told her, and her son, "It's no way to live at all, really."

This time Riley interrupted his mother.

"Then how come you're doin' it?" he asked me.

I looked at him across the table and I couldn't think of anything to tell him that his mother would approve of, so I just told him the truth.

"I don't know," I said, "I guess I haven't found the place where I belong yet."

Riley was sent to bed with a hug from his father and a kiss from his mother and he stopped beside my chair to shake my hand.

"I hope you find your place, Mister."

Coffee was brewed and poured and we drank it at the table and Carol Ann seemed softened by the lateness of the evening. She glanced at me across the table and frowned at my unruly tangle of hair.

"What you need is a haircut," she said, "Most folks around here would be more inclined to give you a ride if you were a clean-cut kid...and if you took that queer earring out of your ear."

Vernon took a slurp from his coffee mug and smiled at his wife.

"Carol Ann was a beautician when I met her," he said, "She still keeps her scissors plenty sharp."

I showered down the hall, my first hot water in days, and when I came back to the kitchen, damp and smelling of soap, Carol Ann sat me down in a chair, draped a sheet across my shoulders and gave me one of the best haircuts I had ever had. She took her time about it and it was relaxing and homey to have someone fuss over my wet curls. When she was finished she showed me a mirror. Behind me in the glass, she looked proud of how she had cleaned me up, but her smile only lasted until I told her I was keeping the earring.

EIGHT
TRUE CONFESSIONS

On Carol Ann's insistence, the three of us stood on the long porch of their house, eyes closed, hands clasped to form a circle, while she spoke aloud what seemed more a condemnation than a prayer. She went on longer than I had heard anyone pray before and when she ran out of every sin and transgression she could imagine, she prayed God's forgiveness and protection from the ones that only He could know and finished with the hope that Jesus would light the pathways of the ignorant and lost; that they might be saved and spared eternal damnation.

She prayed it all in Jesus' name and when I opened my eyes, Carol Ann was looking hard into my face and I wondered had she closed her eyes at all.

"My boy is up at six for school," she said softly, "I'd like it if you were gone away before then."

I told her I would leave early, thanked her once more for supper and the haircut and Vernon walked with me across the dooryard to the tractor shed.

From the porch, as she stepped back inside, Carol Ann hollered after me.

"You're gonna die on that road and burn if you don't come to God, boy."

In the shed, Vernon lit an electric lantern and I rolled out my blankets against a corner of the wall. He lit a cigarette and opened the top of a rollaway toolbox, pulled out a slim silver flask and loosened the cap. He took a long pull from the flask and held it out to me.

"Bourbon," he said.

"Just one," I said, taking the flask and tilting it back. The bourbon was warm and welcome and I lit a Pall Mall to follow it.

We leaned against the plow and smoked and Vernon took another slug or two from the flask, but when he offered it back to me, I waved it away.

"Not a drinkin' man?"

"Not much of one, I guess," I said, "I like my pot, but I never did like feelin' drunk."

Vernon nodded. "Well, you can smoke it out here if you've got some, but wait 'til I go back up to the house so's I don't take the smell with me. Carol Ann would have me up half the night prayin' if she smelled marijuana on me."

I blew cigarette smoke into the dim light of the lantern.

"She won't smell the booze on you?" I asked him, "The bourbon?"

He grinned and shook his head. "You know, Carol Ann's got a knack for spottin' all manner of sin, but she's got an especially good talent for not even noticin' the ones she don't want to see."

I didn't say anything to that. It's one thing to listen when a man criticizes his wife, but it's another thing altogether, a dangerous thing sometimes, to agree with him. I was getting sleepy and my bedroll stretched out invitingly in the corner, but the bourbon had seemed to loosen Vernon's jaw and when he lit a second cigarette, I had one, too.

"Don't take offense at her shooin' you off come morning," he said, "She didn't used to be so hard a woman, or such a religious one, but since we lost our girl, she took to the Bible like it's a stone for throwin' and not a book at all."

For a moment, we were silent and it might have been more uncomfortable than it was if the nighttime song of crickets and frogs hadn't been calling over the farm and fields.

"I shouldn't burden a stranger with my talk," Vernon said quietly, "It's the bourbon, I guess."

I had been quieted by his words, but not burdened by them. I was used to strangers telling me what they might not tell their family or a close friend and I understood that most of the people who picked me up along the highways wanted something from me. Oh, there were those who gave me a ride or a place to sleep just out of kindness alone, but most of them wanted something in return. On the road, everything was some kind of a trade. Mostly, what they wanted was someone to talk to and it stopped surprising me years before what some of them might tell someone just passing through their life; a stranger they knew they would never see again.

"I don't mind it," I said, lighting a third cigarette, "Riley had a sister?"

Vernon sighed and took a long swallow from the flask. He glanced out the wide, open doorway of the tractor shed, across the dooryard where the house sat quiet, but the porch light still glowed and, through a window near the back of the house, a lesser light shined.

"Melissa-Sue. She came two years before Riley," he said, "She took sick three years ago and she was gone in a week."

He tilted the flask to his lips and drank once more then returned it to its hiding place in the toolbox. He turned around to face me and his face was lit by the glow of a match, then another Winston.

"The flu," he whispered, "Just the damned ol' flu, but it took our baby girl down like murder."

I didn't want another smoke, but I could tell that Vernon had more to say before he gave up on the evening and went back to the house, so I rested against the plow blade and lit one more.

"I'm sorry, Vernon," I said quietly, "I'm sorry to hear about your daughter."

From where he stood in the shadows at his workbench, I couldn't see his eyes well enough in the dark to know if he had started to cry, but there was a hitch in his voice when he spoke again.

"An' I'm sorry to tell it," he said, "Hell, I'm drunk enough I shouldn't be talkin' 'bout it at all, botherin' a stranger I took in for a guest."

Vernon didn't know what I knew about the road and how everything that happened was a trade, but not always a bargain. He felt regret for opening up to me about his pain, but he didn't understand that he had bought my ear with his kindness. I had eaten his food, had a shower and a haircut in his home and my bedroll was turned out on the floor of his tractor barn. In accepting what he had to share, I was obliged to let him share his sorrow, too.

"Well, you're telling me about it for one reason or another," I said, "Do you know what it is, Vernon? Why you're tellin' me?"

The bourbon had caught up to him and his words were sluggish and his drawl slipped deeper south.

"I know why. 'Course I know why," he said, "I'm tellin' it to you 'cause I love my wife and I don't want you leavin' here thinkin' poorly of her."

I told him that I didn't think poorly of Carol Ann at all, but he either didn't hear me or just plain didn't believe me. I didn't say it, but I thought that he was talking to himself as much as he was to me.

"Was a time she wasn't so quick to judge and condemn a body," he said, "Oh, she always was a Christian woman, but she didn't used to be so...*mean* about it."

I knew before he told me that the time he was talking about was the time before their little girl had been taken by God and the flu.

"After...she took after The Lord with a vengeance," he said, "She was sure as she could be that her baby girl was dead on account of some sin that *she* had done; or I'd done."

Vernon leaned against the doorframe and looked out across the dooryard, tossed his Winston in the dirt and stubbed it out with the toe of his boot.

"Pastor from the church and all the ladies, too; they tried to tell her it weren't like that, but she wouldn't have no part of it. She didn't *want* God's love an' mercy so she went lookin' for them that preach his fire an' wrath."

He turned around to look at me.

"She started goin' to a new church and she got worse," he said, "But she settled in hard on bein' mean when she started listenin' to that blamed fool preacher on the radio."

I glanced up at him.

"That Old Time Revival show?" I said, "Reverend Johnson Beal?"

Vernon nodded and I was reminded of the bobble-head Jesus on the dashboard of Dalton Cumming's truck.

"That's the man," Vernon said, "You know 'bout him all the way north where you come from?"

I shook my head. "No, no...heard him on the radio comin' south with a trucker. Sounds like a used-car salesman more than he does a preacher."

Vernon spit in the dirt.

"That he does," he said, "That's a kind of man sellin' snake oil and hissin' like one, too. Carol Ann, she sends in money to that show and spends *more* of it goin' round the state to see his church revivals."

He took two crooked steps out of the shed, turned around and stared at me.

"She don't *see* it," he said, "She don't see the way her kind of God is more a devil, but she didn't always act so mean, the way she treated you."

I stepped out of the shed and shook his hand.

"Your wife fed me, Vernon. She cut my long hair, too, and I'm grateful for it."

He grinned.

"Hell, son," he said, "She didn't cut your hair outta any kindness. She only wanted to make you look the way *she* thought you ought to."

He turned toward the house and stumbled across the dooryard. I watched him until he was up on the porch and inside the door and when he closed it behind him, the dog sat on the welcome mat like a guard.

In my blankets, I stayed awake awhile with Vernon's sadness on my mind, but once I slept, I dreamed of lying with Luanna on the river two days earlier. I awoke from the dream, warm and breathing hard, to find that Vernon's dog had crept into the shed to sleep beside me. He lay heavy against my back with his muzzle resting on my shoulder and I thought to shoo him away, but I remembered what Luanna had told me about chasing love away and I let him stay and share my bedroll.

I stroked his fur in the darkness and went back to sleep thinking about the good brown stray sleeping forever in the ground a half-mile away. That dog was dead because of *me*, because I chased his love away with a stone and he would never know that I had given him a name.

Huck.

He had definitely been a Huck, no question about it. I had just been too selfish to see that I was supposed to be his Tom Sawyer

NINE
KENTUCKY WOMAN

I left Vernon's farm in the small hours of the morning, long before the sun or anyone in the house was up. The dog sat and watched me while I rolled up my blankets and neatened up my pack and he let me slip away without barking and waking up his people. It wasn't yet four in the morning and there wouldn't be much traffic when I got to the highway, but I wanted to avoid Carol Ann's righteous stares and viscous prayers. I wanted to avoid Vernon, too, or let him avoid me, in case he was embarrassed or ashamed of the things that he had told me the night before. They had treated me well and taken me in for the night and the only favor I could afford them was to be gone along my way before they woke.

I crossed the damp pasture in darkness and it was darker still in the woods, beneath the trees, but I found my way to the fence-line, then the stream and stood a moment at the mound of Huck's fresh grave. I didn't linger long because it made me feel ashamed, crying at the grave of a dog that was only dead because of me.

"I'm sorry, Huck," I whispered, "That's your name now; Huck."

I slung my pack and crossed the stream to find the highway up ahead and when I reached the top of the slope, I heard a dog's lone bark and I stopped to look and listen. For a moment, I thought I'd see Huck's ghost, bounding up the hill after me, panting and eager to come along, even though I had killed him. Of course, it hadn't been Huck I'd heard, but likely Vernon's hound back on the farm. Huck was gone, forever a stray, and I didn't know if a dog had a soul any more than I knew if a man did, but I knew that wherever he was, he had forgiven me for his murder. Dogs are forgivers by nature; they're better than us that way.

I walked a few miles in the darkness, turning to face the occasional passing car or truck and to show the driver my thumb, but none of them stopped or even slowed down. Beyond the eastern hills, the sun began to rise, but its weak light didn't brighten the day; it pushed grey clouds across the sky and the storm that had lingered overnight in the east blew toward me, threatening rain.

Vernon had told me that the next town was twelve miles south. There would be a diner or a truck stop there, someplace I could wait out the storm with a hot mug of coffee, but I wouldn't make Russellville before the rain came down unless I caught a ride. There was a thick stand of woods along the roadside up ahead and I made up my mind to get off the highway, pitch my tent beneath the cover of a great tree and build a fire. I hadn't slept much the night before, awakened by dreams and the tossing and turning of Vernon's hound, and I hadn't had any coffee. I was hungry, with thirty dollars in my pocket to feed me, and there wouldn't be any food until Russellville, but I thought a day in my dry tent with Huckleberry Finn and my growling stomach seemed a better way to spend the morning than walking all the way into town in the rain. I had a half-full can of Folgers and a small sack of sugar in my pack and three or four mugs of strong coffee would fill the emptiness in my belly, at least until I pissed it all out in some bush.

An old yellow pickup came rattling down the southbound lane, but I didn't hang out my thumb. I had given up on catching a ride, at least for the time being, and set my heart and mind on campfire coffee, but the truck slowed down as it drew up alongside me and the driver laid on the horn.

The truck pulled off on the shoulder just ahead of me and I thought I might change my mind about getting off the road if I had a ride all the way into Russellville. Instead of tossing my gear in the back of the truck and climbing in on the passenger side, I went to the driver's window to ask about how far they could take me.

The driver was rolling down the window as I drew near and, in the side-mounted mirror, I saw a woman's face, or at least a woman's chin and cheek and the fall of long brown hair. I shrugged my duffel bag off of my shoulder, leaned to look inside the cab of the truck and found a familiar face.

"Carol Ann..." I said.

Vernon's wife sat behind the steering wheel, wearing a plain blue dress and a thin wool coat pulled across her shoulders. For a moment, she stared out the windshield at the highway, but then she looked at me without expression and took a brown paper sack from beside her on the seat. She held it out to me and I took it.

"I won't give you any ride," she said, "But it wasn't right to send you off like that, without something to eat."

I bent to stuff the paper bag beneath the flaps of my pack and when I straightened, I looked her in the eye and thanked her.

"That's a good lunch there," she said, "Four pork sandwiches and two apples. There's milk, but you'll wanna drink that before it gets warm."

I thanked her again and I expected her to put the truck in gear and head back to her farm, but she glanced back out the windshield and then straight back at me.

Here comes the trade. Now, I'll find out what she wants from me; the price of her apples and pork.

She sighed and her mouth turned down, but her eyes stayed steady on my own.

"I know Vernon talked to you last night," she said, "I could smell the bourbon on him when he come to bed and Vernon likes to talk too much when he's drunk; long as he's got anyone besides me to talk to, I guess."

I nodded and I thought before I spoke, knowing that the more I told her, the more expensive my lunch would come out to be. Everything's a trade; nothing's ever a bargain.

"Yes, ma'am. He did talk to me some."

Her eyes narrowed, just the smallest bit, but I didn't think she was getting angry. I thought she was paying close attention.

"Well..." she said after a moment, "Ain't you gonna tell me what he told."

I didn't answer her in a hurry, but I thought back on all that her husband had said to me and I realized that if I gave her just the fewest of his words, I could also give her the biggest truth of them, too.

"Mostly, he told me that he loves you."

Her eyes widened ever so slightly, but the corners of her mouth drew down that much tighter.

"I know my husband well," she said, "He didn't spend the best part of an hour romanticizin' over *me*."

I shrugged.

"Well, he maybe took the long way gettin' around to it," I told her, "But that's what he wanted me to know."

"He told you more than that," she said, "He told you 'bout Melissa-Sue, didn't he?"

I looked away from her and I shoved my hands in the pockets of my jeans.

"Carol Ann...ma'am...I don't wanna..."

She interrupted me with a wave of her hand and I was grateful that she had.

"Never mind it," she said, "I guess I didn't come out here to make you tell me what I already know. I come out here to find you so I can tell you somethin' myself."

I looked up from the dirt and found her eyes.

"Whatever Vernon said about me might be true," she said softly, "I'm a hard woman of God and I'm not easy to live around, but I got my own punishment to live through."

I didn't speak. I just stared.

"You know something about that yourself, don'tcha?" she said, "About livin' in the judgement of The Lord?"

She was right about me, at least as right as a stranger could be. I was living through my punishment, walking off my sins, but I didn't blame it on God, at least not anymore. I stopped blaming God when I stopped believing in Him and I named my life a curse and blamed it on myself.

"Ain't that what's got you out here on the road?" she said, "You're payin' a livin' wage for some sin."

"I don't believe in sin," I told her, "I just...I wanted to be alone."

Carol Ann smiled, but it was sad, and gruesome in a way.

"And you're *still* alone," she said, "Exiled as surely as Cain was cast away into the land of Nod.

Only, you're too prideful to know it's God who exiled you, so you think you done it to yourself."

I didn't argue back. As sure as Vernon had bought my ear with his kindness the night before, Carol Ann had done the same and I was obliged to stand on the roadside with the first drops of rain falling down on my shoulders and listen to her judgements and her confession, too.

"I come to tell you that I see it; why you live like you do, and I ain't one to judge it when it's God who willed it so."

"No disrespect, ma'am, but you seemed to judge me last night at your table."

"That's what I come to say," she told me, "I'm hard to live around and I know my husband, and maybe even my boy...they must think sometimes about runnin' off and leavin' me alone."

Tears brimmed in her eyes, but they refused to fall.

"I couldn't have you sittin' there in my own kitchen," she said, "Makin' out how easy it is for a boy to just up and go; not in front of my man and 'specially not in front of my son."

It was hard to look at her, but I did, and in her eyes, I found her fear of being left behind; alone in the house where her daughter had died, alone with her punishing God and her sin.

"Ain't you got a momma somewhere?" she asked me, "Ain't you got folks worryin' over you?"

"My mother's dead," I said.

"I s'pose I know that's what you're bein' punished for," she said, "You either killed her or you think you done it."

Carol Ann dropped the truck into gear and left me standing on the edge of the highway and I stood there long enough to let the rain wash my tears away from my face.

TEN
EXILE

I made camp in the cradle of two tall trees and their boughs kept most of the rain off my tent and out of my fire. I used the last of the water in my canteen for coffee and while I waited on it to boil, I ate two of the sandwiches Carol Ann had given me and chased them down with the milk.

You'll wanna drink that before it gets warm.

The day remained dim and the clouds lay low in the sky, muffling the sounds from the highway when the occasional truck blew by in the rain. The coffee was strong and after it was gone, I got stoned and stretched out in my tent with Mark Twain's greatest story, tapping cigarette ashes into an old tin can while I read. I left the tent flap open to the cool of the day and my campfire burned itself out against the rain and the breeze.

I had meant to read myself to sleep, to chase Huck and Jim down the Mississippi and then into a dream, but I couldn't get lost on the river because my mind kept drifting back to the road. I closed the book, stowed it away in my pack and sat in the open flap of the tent. I lit a cigarette and smoked and every now and again, the breeze tossed a light mist of rain across my face.

There's something about a road, something mysterious and mystical paved into the earth and left there to outlive the people who built it. I never tried to explain it to anyone who didn't already know it, because it's a strange idea to speak out, but I think the blacktop remembers all the lives that ever rolled over it, every person or good dog that ever died out on it. I suppose most people can get out on a road and think of it as no more than some great dead thing meant to take them where they're going and lead them back again, but it's *more* than that. If you ever lived out on the road, the way I did, then you learned that it was alive and sometimes deadly, and that it could change its shape and take you places unexpected.

I knew the interstates and I used them sometimes, but mostly I stuck to the state highways and county two-lanes. The interstates passed through towns without touching them, stretched from city to city with no connection to the places in between, or the people. They were built for a world that moved fast and I seldom had a reason to hurry so I avoided the bright freeways and kept to leftover roads that took me places where time slowed down and sometimes even stood still.

Some roads were like rivers and some were like snakes and sometimes a road could be both at once, depending on who was riding on it. For one man, a stretch of blacktop is a way back home and for another, that same road might be his last escape and a fast way out of nowhere. I had been a long time on the road and come to know it well enough to hear some of the spirits buried beneath it, but the highway just beyond the trees was a strange one. It seemed older than it was, maybe even ancient, and wiser than a road should ever be. I sat a stone's throw from the asphalt, listening through the rain for the sound of the highway and I was almost certain it was listening just as closely for me; listening and waiting.

You're gonna die on that road and burn if you don't come to God.

There was something out there waiting down that road for me and I didn't know what it was, but I feared it. Most roads are such a part of the earth that you can ride them all night long under Heaven and only see sky. *This* road seemed like the kind of road where God might go out walking, and I wondered if He knew that I had shed some blood upon it. He might not have seen me do it Himself, but the devil surely had and may have told Him.

This road felt like the kind where the devil walks, too. The trouble for me when it came to God and Satan was that I had never been good at telling one from the other.

I reminded myself that I didn't believe in either of them and wrapped myself up in the folds of my blankets. I fell asleep wondering what it proved if I were right; and what I'd do if I were wrong about God and the devil, too.

Would I know them if I met them on the highway?

I dreamed of the road, but I was somewhere farther down its spine and Huck was with me, still alive and smiling. We were out in the storm, but the rain had turned to dust, and I couldn't see the highway just a sign out on its edge. I couldn't read the sign in the blowing storm, but the wind whipped it back and forth on its post and it made a rattling clang like a warning.

Out of the dust, came a car so dark that I couldn't even see it, just its headlights in the haze. It pulled off of the highway, crushing earth beneath its tires, but it didn't sound like gravel; more like brittle, crunching bones. I looked inside to see the driver, but there was just a faceless shadow. The passenger's side door handle gleamed, even though there wasn't any moonlight in the storm.

Huck tucked his tail and tensed low to the ground, laid back his ears and growled deep in his throat. He barked fearfully, furiously at the phantom car and when I reached out to open the door and climb in, he leapt from the ground and bit my hand, drawing blood.

The car sped away and was lost in the storm and I turned to scold Huck for his bite, but he was gone. I called his name in the darkness, but he didn't answer with a bark or come to my side.

Huck? C'mon, boy...c'mon, Huck!

The moon slipped loose from the clouds and the dust blew away on the wind and I could see the highway, black but stained with blood. Huck lay dead on the broken white line and my hand felt heavy. I looked to see if the bite was bad and found no marks or blood, just a smooth black stone clutched in my palm.

I awoke in a panic, my heart racing hard and my breath so sharp and shallow that I almost couldn't catch it. The day was still grey and the rain fell hard on my tent, but when I pulled back the flap for a look at the storm, I was relieved to see the sky was leaking water, not dry dust.

ELEVEN
NASHVILLE STARS

By early evening, I was back out on the roadside, hanging my thumb out for every passing car while the storm held its breath overhead. I didn't stand still and count on a ride; I walked along the shoulder making time instead of wasting it. I hadn't walked long, maybe half an hour, when a car rolled up slow beside me and paced me. It was a primer grey Camaro with more dents than curves and country music oozing out its windows.

For a moment, I remembered the dream and the sound of Huck's frantic barking, but when I turned to look in the car, there was no shadow shape behind the wheel, just a long-haired kid wearing a cowboy hat, a cigarette dangling from his friendly grin.

"Where you walkin' to?" he hollered.

"Memphis."

He laughed and stopped the car.

"Get on in, man," he said, "Give them boots a rest."

I stowed my gear on the backseat next to a guitar case and got in the front with the long-haired cowboy. He reached across the cab and we shook hands.

"Can you get me as far as Russellville?" I asked him.

"*Russellville*? Buddy, I can take you all the way as far as Nashville, Tennessee."

The Camaro looked like hell, but it ran just fine, growling like a hungry beast when the kid pulled it back onto the blacktop. He drove fast and we sped southeast through occasional fits of rain, thick guitars twanging from the stereo speakers and the smoke from cigarettes and pot slipping out the windows on the wind.

The kid kept time with the music, tapping silver rings and slapping his palm on the steering wheel, and he sang along to every song. He had a great voice, smooth and rich and strong and when he sang he sounded older than he was.

He glanced at me, still grinning and smoking and nodded toward the dashboard tape deck.

"You like Steve Earle?" he asked me.

"Never heard of him."

Every once in a while, I would catch a ride with someone who might have become a friend, if I wanted one and we hadn't met on the road. That long-haired kid with the beautiful voice was one of that kind and we became fast friends, at least for the short time we would know each other, and we passed the two-hour ride getting acquainted and getting stoned.

He was close to my age at twenty-three and no stranger to the road, either. He told me he had been traveling between his hometown in northern Kentucky and Nashville since he was seventeen, first by thumb or Greyhound bus and, more recently, in the torn bucket seat of the banged-up Camaro. In Nashville, he slept in his car, played music on the streets and shopped his demo tape around to anyone who might pay him to sing; bar owners, record labels, radio program directors. He likened himself to the singer on the stereo, Steve Earle, and said he wanted to write songs like his and make country records with loud drums and fat guitars.

"I'm a rock and roll kid," he told me, "But I'm born and raised in the sticks."

I liked the album we had been listening to. Guitar Town, it was called. It reminded me of a lot of the older country music that my mother liked to listen to, but it also reminded me of another singer.

"He reminds me of Springsteen," I said, "Something about his songs..."

The hippie cowboy nodded and smacked his hand against his thigh.

"Exactly that!" he said, "Steve Earle says this whole album come about on account of him seein' a Bruce Springsteen concert."

"No shit?"

"No shit at all," he said, "I read that right in Rolling Stone magazine. I shoulda figured you for a Springsteen fan, bein' from New Jersey an' all."

I told him about the Springsteen cassettes in my duffel bag and he laughed and nodded when I said they were the only tapes I took with me when I left home.

"I like ol' Bruce," he said, "He's got a lot of country in him, you know, for a northern guy."

"I like him more since I've been on the road than I ever did before," I said, "Sometimes, his music means *everything* to me."

"Hey, I get it, man," he said, "You wanna pop one in the tape deck? We already heard guitar Town four times."

I leaned over the seat and dug through my pack for my cassettes and I skipped over the obvious one, the one I was sure the kid had heard, and chose my favorite one; the one with Springsteen looking bleary and burned out, staring hard at nothing, standing in front of a set of blinds, drawn closed over a window to keep out the darkness; or to keep it in.

I slid it into the cassette deck, there was a burst of drums and Bruce Springsteen and the E Street Band carried us from the county highway to the big interstate and we came upon the bright lights of Nashville listening to Darkness on the Edge of Town.

The evening had gone full dark and the city lights spread out before us like a glittering sea. Nashville was bigger than I had imagined it and I was disappointed that the reality of it didn't size up with the small-town expectations I had from growing up seeing *The Grand Ol' Opry* and *Hee Haw* on television. Nashville was a big city and I didn't want any part of it.

On the northern outskirts of the city, the kid pulled the car off the interstate and followed an exit to a quiet road in a thin neighborhood of small houses.

"I can let you off here, if you wanna keep on hitchin' or go into the city," he said, "But there's a camp back a-ways down this road, right up on the river. There's a bunch of us that stay around there."

I glanced at him, then up at the freeway and thought it over.

"Hell, you ought to come and crash tonight," he said, "We ain't wild or nothin' like that, but we get stoned and play music. You ever play any music?"

I grinned, embarrassed.

"I got a couple harmonicas," I said, "But I ain't much good."

The kid grinned back at me.

"That settles it," he said, "Whatta you say?"

I said it sounded better than standing on the freeway on the outskirts of Nashville all night long and he turned the Camaro down the road and followed the curve of the Cumberland River. We came to an overgrown dirt track and he slowed and let the car crawl down the slope and through the trees to the river's edge.

The tramp camp was a circle of cars, vans and tents, with a big fire burning in the center, that reminded me of my season with the carnival. I saw a dozen or so people, some sitting around the fire, some washing clothes in a big metal tub and others playing music and getting stoned. Some were young, still in their teens, and there were a few grey-bearded old men among them, too. A beautiful black-haired girl in a white dress and boots rushed toward us, passed me over with a smile and wrapped her arms around the long-haired kid.

"Henry Hutchins!" she said, "I thought you'd *never* get back."

Henry Hutchins. Two hours in the car and we never said our names.

We left the Camaro clicking and cooling in the shadow of a great wide Oak and the pretty girl hugged me, too, but nowhere near as enthusiastically as she had embraced Henry Hutchins, and the three of us walked together to the camp. No one questioned my presence and everyone welcomed me in.

There was soup from a big brass pot and coarse bread that was soft and warm if you drenched it in the broth. We drank beer, but no hard liquor, and after two cans of Budweiser, I switched to a bottle of soda before I got too drunk; but not before I got drunk enough to dance.

Almost everybody in camp played an instrument and even the ones who didn't could sing.

All of us were stoned and most of us were drunk and in the wooded shadows on the river's edge, guitars and banjos came to life and a blue-haired girl bowed a fiddle while a black boy took his drumsticks to a sawed-off hunk of tree trunk.

Sweet, clear voices sang in the darkness; old country, blues and hymns and they did a jangly version of John Fogerty's Proud Mary and none of them seemed to realize that *they* were the people in the song. If they did realize it, that they were "the people who live," they sang it without pride or sense of self and it swept me to my feet among the ones who chose to dance.

I had learned how to dance from my mother when I was a boy; late night lessons on the living room carpet to Elvis, Buddy Holly and The Everly Brothers. She taught me how to do the twist to Chubby Checker and how to two-step to Mickey Gilley, but one day I got old enough to be self-conscious and I only ever danced when I was alone; unless I was drunk.

That night, I had enough of a buzz to kick my boots up and dance and I spun with a girl in pigtails through a haze of dust and smoke. Across the river, the big city lights were bright and offensive, but here on the wooded bank there was only the glow of the fire. The music slowed and we danced close and it was nice to hold someone and to be held, too, with a fiddle sighing underneath the trees like a hillbilly breeze.

The fire burned low, the music softened and the dancers drifted to the ground and sat still. I played harmonica on a dare and an old man with a harp of his own taught me a simple, chugging rhythm and two high notes that sounded just like a train. Henry Hutchins played a song he wrote, about a town that caught on fire every weekend. I listened close to the words he sang and was rewarded with a fine short story and a chorus that could kick your ass. He was a handsome kid who could play and sing and I thought one day he'd be a star.

In all of the years since then, I never heard his name on the radio or saw his picture in a record shop, but I always had the feeling that, if he was alive, Henry Hutchins was playing his guitar somewhere.

A few hours before dawn, we all drifted off, alone or in pairs, to sleeping bags and tents or backseats. Henry and the girl in the long white dress laughed all the way to his Camaro and you could still hear them giggling with the windows rolled up.

I was alone with the last of the fire and the girl I had danced with, but now that the music had ended, we sat in awkward silence. I lit a cigarette and she bummed one and we stared at the fire and smoked.

"You wanna fool around some?" she said.

I took a deep drag on the Pall Mall and blew out the smoke on a sigh.

"You gonna get mad if I say I don't really want to?" I said, "Or you just wanna do it 'cause you're bored."

She blushed and smiled and I realized that she was very pretty and probably only about fifteen years old.

"I guess because I'm bored and kinda drunk," she said, "Anyway, Amanda snatched up Henry Hutchins before he even got outta his car."

Ouch.

"Oh, gosh, I didn't mean that the way it come out," she said, "You're nice, too."

"Well, you're too young for me to mess around with," I told her, "And you're too young for Henry, too."

She sighed and when she did, she looked away.

"I know I am," she whispered, "But I feel like I've been around for a long, long time."

I sat with her awhile and we passed my pipe between us and she got over wanting to kiss and settled for someone to talk with. Her name was Katy and she had barely turned sixteen, but she'd run away from home three months before and come all the way from West Virginia.

"It ain't really runnin' away, though," she sighed, "Not if nobody there wants you back."

I knew exactly how she felt and that she was right.

She said her father was a drinker and she didn't trust his hands. Sometimes he beat her or touched her where it shamed her; where it should have shamed *him*, but didn't.

"I told my mother once and she slapped my face for lyin' and I seen in her eyes that she already knew what he'd done."

She almost cried, but instead she sang a ballad soft and low, about a broken promise and a crooked cross. She sang with a southern sorrow and a sweetness, too, and I wondered when she closed her eyes, did she disappear or did the world?

I glanced across the river at the city skyline.

"You should be over there," I said, "Singin' on a stage."

Katy sighed as softly as she'd sang and said, "Don't look over there; look up at the sky."

I stared up through the trees, beyond the thinning clouds into the clear night sky and Katy leaned against my shoulder and looked up, too.

"Them's the only Nashville stars you're gonna see around here."

TWELVE
SHADOWBOXING HEAVEN

First, I heard the birds and the sound of the river, then the rest of the daytime noises; traffic on the highway and a bell out on the water, the bang and clang of something big being built in the city and the hum of a harmonica, soft, but very near. I opened my eyes to a day still in the dark, but the coals of the fire had been rekindled and the air smelled of smoke and coffee.

The camp was still asleep, except for the old man who had taught me how to blow my harp like a freight train. He sat beside the fire, a steaming mug beside him in the dirt and the flickering glow of the flames reflected in the chrome of his harmonica.

I rolled out of my blankets, pulled on my boots and dug in my pack for the tin cup I carried with me. I stowed away my bedroll, shouldered my pack and joined the old man at the fire. I asked him if I could share his coffee and he nodded toward the pot.

"You been travelin' a long time now, ain'tcha?" he said.

I filled my cup and burned my lips on the first sip.

"Yeah...almost four years," I said, "How can you tell?"

The old man slipped his harmonica into the pocket of his flannel shirt and smiled. He didn't have a single tooth in his head, but his smile was warm and honest.

"Oh, lots of little tells," he said, "But mostly because you were smart enough to have your own cup."

I laughed. When I first hit the road, I had no idea what I should carry. I packed my clothes and my notebook, a tube of toothpaste and my Springsteen tapes. I would have left my hometown without a blanket to sleep on if my childhood friend Ray Laws hadn't insisted, when I stopped over to tell him goodbye, that I take along his sleeping bag. I had learned a lot in three years and I carried canned food and coffee, a makeshift pot to cook in and a bowl, spoon and cup.

I learned the hard way that a lot of people were willing to share their coffee or stew, but they might not have a cup or a spoon to lend.

"I wake you up with my harmonica?" he said, "I like to play in the mornin' time, but I play soft and low and ain't ever woke anyone up around here."

I shook my head.

"No. I wake up early when I'm outside," I told him, "I heard the birds before I heard your song."

He took a sip from his mug and bummed one of my cigarettes. I leaned in to give him a light and he took a deep drag and exhaled with a toothless grin.

"I *do* like a store-bought smoke," he said, "I mostly roll my own; when I can afford a sack o' tobacco, I mean."

I dug in the flaps of my duffel bag. I had a half-full pouch of Topps rolling tobacco that I kept for times when I didn't have any money for cigarettes. I dug it out and offered it to the old man. He showed me his toothless smile when I handed it to him.

"Thank you, boy," he said, "But you're sure you can spare it?"

I told him I could and I thanked him for the harmonica lesson the night before. I wanted to shoulder my gear and get back out on the highway by the time the sun came up.

"You buggin' out then?" the old man asked me.

"Yes, Sir," I said, "I wanna try and make Memphis by tonight."

He nodded and glanced up at me.

"You mind if I say a prayer over you before you go?"

I sighed.

"I know it's rude," I said, "But I'd rather you didn't, if that's alright. I've had about all the praying I can stand the last couple of days."

The old man grinned.

"It ain't rude of you," he said, "But what you got against it, if you know your reason?"

I hitched the duffel bag's strap higher up my shoulder and lit another cigarette. I took my time answering the old man's question, took deep pulls from the Pall Mall and looked down at him through the smoke.

"I know my reason," I said, "Me and God; we've been fighting each other...for a long time."

The old man laughed so hard that he choked on his cigarette, but he laughed right through it until he was wheezing.

"Is that so?" he said, "You fancy yourself like Jacob, do you? Wrestlin' angels and such?"

"No, sir. I wrestle demons, too."

He leaned toward me, rested his hands on his knees, and the cigarette waggled between his lips when he spoke.

"Well, I'll tell you this much, son," he said, "You're the only dog in *that* fight."

"How so?"

He laughed again, but not as hard as he had a moment before and he didn't choke or wheeze.

"You're just shadowboxin' Heaven," he said, "God ain't fightin' you *back* or you'd be *dead*."

THIRTEEN
NOBODY RIDES FOR FREE

It took me six short rides and most of the morning to get beyond the outskirts of West Nashville. That's just the way it was, hitching around a city. Most of the traffic around a bigger city is local and rides are hard to catch when people are in a hurry or on their way to work, but by noon I had managed to get around the city, off of the interstate and onto U.S. Highway 70.

I might have gotten to Memphis sooner if I had stayed out on the 40, but *'The Road'* can mean the highway you roll over or it can be the journey that you're *on*. The interstate seemed like a detour, a rolling hive of strangers, but the 70 felt familiar; a road that knew the way back to the mystery out there waiting.

The storm that had been dogging me all the way from Ohio had thinned and spread out to the south, where it piled up against the green horizon and gathered its strength. Straggling clouds passed overhead, but they didn't so much as spit, so I walked awhile along the highway with the sun warm on my back and my Walkman on my belt.

I kept the headphone volume low enough that I could still hear the traffic over Springsteen bellowing about being born down in a dead man's town, but I must have had it up just a little too loud. Behind me, an air-horn blasted and, for just a moment, I mistook it for the honk of a saxophone, but then it sounded again and I heard a big rig groaning down through its gears. I was startled enough to hurry farther off the roadside, but I hadn't been in any danger of being run over. A big green Kenworth huffed to a stop, left wheels in the breakdown lane, right ones crunching up dust in the soft dirt on the roadside.

It was a beautiful thing, as far as trucks go; a big, extended cab with a fancy two-tone paint job and chrome rims on all eighteen wheels. That Kenworth might have been the cleanest truck I had ever seen, if it hadn't been streaked with mud and water spots from the storm. Still, the sun sparkled on the rims and other chrome attachments. I took off the headphones, gripped a gleaming rail, climbed up on the shining step-side and yanked the big door open.

I swung my pack from my shoulder to the floorboard, pulled myself up into the cab and settled in the passenger's seat, squeezing my legs around my gear. I turned to the driver and we shook hands.

"Thanks a lot," I said, "I'm headed for Memphis."

He looked to be in his late sixties and he was remarkably thin. His work shirt hung loose on narrow shoulders and his skin was nearly as grey as his hair. He sat hunched in the big seat, leaning into the steering wheel.

"I can get you to Memphis," he told me, "But before I drop it in gear, let's have us a meetin' of the minds."

I nodded.

"First thing is, this ain't no free ride," he said, "You know how to handle a pallet-jack, kid?"

I nodded a second time. I hadn't known what a pallet-jack was three years earlier, but since then I had loaded and off-loaded enough trailers to know how to work one.

"Sure, I do," I said, "I've lumped plenty of freight."

"That's good then," the trucker said, "You willin' to do a little workin' on the way to Memphis?"

I was.

"Yes, sir," I said, "Willing and able."

It was the driver's turn to nod and it came with a grin.

"That's the thing right there," he said, "I ain't always so able as I used to be. I got a fiery pain in my back and down my legs and I'm straight worn out. It's about all I can do just drivin' this truck."

"That sounds bad," I said, "Just leave the freight to me; no problem."

He raised his arm and aimed his thumb back toward the trailer and a flash of pain shut his eyes and tightened his jaw.

"I got two stops between here and Memphis and one more when we get there," he said, "They're heavy pallets. You lump 'em all and I'll throw you fifty dollars and lunch on top of the ride."

I hadn't expected him to offer me any wages and I would have done the work in exchange for the ride, but the money sounded fair and I was hungry. I still had the thirty dollars from Luanna tucked in my jeans, but I didn't even know if that would be enough to get me inside the gates of Graceland and I needed to stock up on canned goods and smokes. I needed batteries, too, for my Walkman.

"Deal," I grinned, offering my hand again.

"There's one last thing," the driver said.

"What's that?"

He sighed.

"That's a big knife there on your hip," he said, "I seen it when you climbed in. You the kind to start trouble?"

I glanced down at the scuffed leather sheathe hanging from my belt, strapped to my thigh with a leather chord; the black and silver pommel, waiting for my hand if I should need it.

"No, sir," I promised, "I can stow it in my bag or you could hold on to it, if it makes you nervous."

The skinny trucker laughed and, for a moment, his eyes brightened and his face flushed with color.

"Son, I got a gun right here that'll blow a hole through *three* of you."

I stared at him.

"But you don't look like the kind of boy I'd have to kill," he said, "So don't you worry none about that."

He shifted out of neutral and the big Kenworth rocked and lurched forward, back out on the highway, bound for Memphis. We traded names and his was Lonnie James. Over the next few minutes and miles, he told me the story of his life.

He had come home from the second world war with two skills, killing men and driving truck, and he took a job in his hometown hauling livestock all over Texas. He bought his first truck in 1953 and went nationwide, working for himself, moving freight coast to coast and living out of truck stops. He never married or had any children and he was dying the way he had lived, alone behind the wheel of his rig.

"I got the cancer in my bones," he said, "Doctor says I won't see a year."

I looked at him. Now that I knew what it was, I could see the cancer, even though it was lurking deep in his bones. It showed itself in the color of his skin, the starkness of his eyes and the pained way he bent over the steering wheel as he drove. I had felt it in his tired grip when we shook hands and heard it in his voice when he confessed it.

"But you keep on driving," I said.

He glanced across the cab and tossed me a slow wink.

"You know what they say, son" he grinned, "Keep on truckin'."

We kept on truckin' west out of Nashville, rolling past towns and open fields, listening to drivers crackling over the CB and a country music station on the radio that played mostly old songs, the records my mother used to play; Johnny Cash, Hank Williams, Loretta Lynn. I thought about the gypsy musicians camped on the outskirts of Nashville, especially Henry Hutchins and Katy and hoped they would have their days on the radio, too. They had the talent for it, and they had enough hurt for it, too.

Lonnie spoke about his sickness and his looming death without ever mentioning God, but there were markers along the roadside, left there by The Lord or His people, to remind us that this was still *His* country and He'd come this way before us. There were tall white crosses planted hard in empty fields, rusted metal signs hung from barbed-wire fences to remind us 'Jesus Saves' and churches in the towns and in between them.

At an intersection, Lonnie slowed the rig for a flashing yellow light and we saw a great black raven perched atop a highway sign. The dark bird flapped its wings and stretched up tall on legs like twigs, but it didn't fly away in fear. It stood firm on its watch post, fixed its steely black eyes on us and cawed against the roar of the big diesel motor.

Lonnie shook his head as we blew by the bird and I watched it in the side-view mirror, still flapping its wings and screaming silently after us.

"I know it sounds hokey," Lonnie said, "But I been seein' them ravens more and more since I got sick."

I glanced at him and hoped my grin didn't look too gruesome.

"That's just in your head," I told him, "You're probably just noticing them more now, than you did before."

Lonnie laughed, but it came out cackling and I wondered if he knew that he sounded just like a crow.

"They been noticin' *me*, too," he sighed, "Them birds; they know carrion when they see it."

A few miles farther on, we passed another roadside church, a big Pentecostal outpost with an old fashion bell out in front and a big sign planted beside it.

I felt about that sign the way Lonnie had felt about the raven and I mumbled under my breath.

"The Good Reverend gets around."

Lonnie cocked his ear my way.

"What's that?"

I waved his question away with a lie.

"Nothing," I said, "Just singin' along with the radio."

FOURTEEN
LUMPING FREIGHT

At a warehouse in a small town called Camden, Lonnie expertly backed the trailer up against the loading dock and reached across the cabin with the freight manifest in his hand.

"You know what to do with this?"

"Yeah, I do," I said, "I'll bring it back signed."

I climbed down from the truck and went around the corner of the warehouse to the receiving office and handed the manifest over to a woman at the desk. She read over the manifest and looked up at me.

"Where's Lonnie?"

"He's stayin' in the truck," I told her, "He's not feelin' very good, I guess."

She frowned and shook her head.

"It's a shame," she said, "A good man like him sufferin' so."

I nodded and took the manifest back with her signature on it and she pointed me through a door that led to the warehouse and the loading dock.

"Jack or Wayne will meet you with the forklift," she said, "Just make sure they sign off on the delivery when you're done."

It was hot in the trailer and I worked up an hour's worth of sweat spinning pallets out of the stack and wheeling them to the end of the trailer so Wayne could pick them up with the forklift and haul them across the warehouse. My shirt was drenched and my hair was, too, and when I took the manifest to Wayne for his initials, he reached inside a rattling old refrigerator and handed me a cold bottle of RC cola.

When I took the manifest back to the truck, Lonnie was asleep behind the wheel, but he woke up when I pulled the door shut behind me and reached for the paperwork. He looked it over and nodded at me.

"You got that done faster than I expected," he said, "Got the paperwork all signed proper, too."

He cranked the key, the Kenworth rumbled to life and rocked across the dirt yard to the gate. We crawled a few blocks to the highway and Lonnie pointed the truck's nose west.

"There's a truck stop just up ahead," he said, "Best steak sandwiches in the state. You can order whatever you want, o' course, but the steak sandwich is damned good."

We sat at the DRIVERS ONLY counter and we both had the steak sandwich with thick wedge-cut fries and tall glasses of iced tea. A lot of the truckers knew Lonnie and the waitresses did, too, and they fussed over him. When our sandwiches were gone, one of them brought us thick slabs of peach cobbler with thick whipped cream.

"Dessert's on the house," she smiled, "And don't you argue with me 'bout it, Lonnie."

Lonnie didn't argue, but he added a few more dollar bills to the tip he had tucked under a sugar bowl and he kissed her on the cheek on his way out the door. I followed him out and had a smoke before we climbed back into the truck.

"I used to date that gal," he told me, "The one who brought us the cobbler."

"What happened to that?" I asked him.

"She started *lovin'* me."

We spent 40 minutes at a warehouse in Jackson and by the time I unloaded the last of the pallets on the outskirts of Memphis, the day was leaning on evening and I was exhausted. Lonnie handed me a crisp fifty-dollar bill and offered to drop me off on his way back to the highway. We were in an industrial area near the city, but there was an open field across the road from the warehouse, with a few thin trees clustered in a far corner. It looked like a good enough place to sleep and Lonnie and I parted ways with a handshake.

The sky was still mostly clear and the storm still faraway in the southwest, so I didn't bother pitching the tent. I got a little stoned, smoked a cigarette and fell asleep on my bedroll to the sounds of the highway. It was whispering something that sounded *almost* like my name.

It was storming again, in the dream that I had, and Huck was stranded with me on a highway in the dark, with the dust pouring hard from the sky and piling up on the road. The wind howled down the center line, bringing trash on its dusty breath; old cans and wrinkled wrappers and a bald black tire, too.

Huck hunched and growled at dim lights on the highway and a long, dark car came purring out of the dust, like a black cat sneaking down the road. I knew we had been there before, but I had no idea where we were or how we had come there.

Huck's dead.

He *wasn't* dead, though; he was right there beside me in the dust storm, barking and growling at the driver of the ghostly car. I remembered the car and that Huck had bitten me to keep me from opening its door. He growled deeper and bared his teeth when I bent to look into the car.

Elvis Presley sat behind the wheel, clean in a pink and black suit, smiling through darkness and dust. He had one arm draped across the back of the seat and the other dangled cool over the steering wheel He wasn't the grey, bloated King who had died eight years before, but the young, rocking prince whose ghost would live forever.

He flashed that famous sidelong grin and nodded toward the shadowed back seat.

"Look who I found, baby."

In the back seat, slim in a smooth blue dress, tall in a cocked black hat, my mother sat stiff and straight in the shadowy dust, a clutch of daisies on her lap. She was young, too; a woman I recognized only from a photograph and her long leather jacket made a creaky sound when she leaned in to smile at me.

"You better get home, Richie."

Huck was barking wildly and bounding back and forth between me and the car, but Elvis slipped me a wink and slapped the front seat.

"C'mon an' get on in now, Teddy Bear," he said, "Momma says it's time to go home."

I reached for the door handle. Huck snarled.

"He doesn't want me to," I told Elvis, "Huck doesn't want me to get in the car."

Elvis winked again and curled up his lip, but I didn't trust his dimples; not for a second.

"Now, don't pay no mind to what ol' Huck thinks," he said, "He ain't nothin' but a hound dog."

The King blasted his mystery car's horn, my mother shrieked in the back seat and Huck ran out onto the highway, whining in the dirty fog.

The car roared away and blew the dusty haze away from the ground at my feet and I realized I was standing on a fresh mound of earth, a cedar board headstone leaning in the dirt.

FIFTEEN
DISGRACELAND

In Memphis the next morning, I washed up and changed clothes in the men's room of a Trailways station and paid eight quarters to stash my gear in a locker downstairs in the depot. I splurged on a late breakfast from the bus station café; runny eggs with biscuits and gravy and a thin sausage patty, fried too crisp. I played a dollar's worth of songs on the jukebox, ate breakfast fast and lingered over coffee and a cigarette.

Getting to Graceland was as easy as hailing a cab out in front of the bus station. I almost never took a taxi anywhere, but I had found out from the waitress working the café counter that it was going to cost a lot less than I had expected to get into the mansion, so I settled in the back of a yellow cab for a ride out Elvis Presley Boulevard.

I admit that sometimes I expect too much from a road, but the one named for The King of Rock and Roll was one that had been paved in my imagination and the reality of it was underwhelming. I expected a pastoral country road, a tree-lined strip of memory and magic winding through time to a secluded estate where a king once reigned. I had always imagined that Elvis had lived out in the country, but it was a short ride through Memphis, past liquor stores and cheap motels and auto shops. I thought the road might redeem itself the nearer we got to Graceland, but it only cheapened itself with souvenir stands and name-dropping sandwich shops.

Graceland's famous gates, with musical notes and twin effigies of Elvis molded right into the iron, stood wide-open to the world. Tour buses cruised the tree-lined driveway, but the cabbie let me out on the street and I had a smoke on the sidewalk before I went in to find a ticket.

Beyond the gates, a winding drive edged a green slope on its way to the mansion on the hill. I had never had enough money to be impressed by it and I hadn't seen enough mansions to judge one against another. Graceland stood in a grove of oaks, a tall house with four great columns and a gabled roof, and it was neither intimidating or inviting. It was the kind of house that I would never sleep in, a house built to look down on me; one I'd have to pay to set foot inside of.

I shared the sidewalk with groups of pilgrims disguised as tourists, some of them posing for pictures and others weeping at the gates, and I remembered a story that Bruce Springsteen told about jumping the wall at Graceland, to meet Elvis and give him a song. He had been intercepted by guards who told him Presley wasn't home and sent him away and I wondered how the ghost of Elvis felt about his gates standing open all day, *especially* when he was home.

The day I was there, Elvis Presley was home. He was home now *every* day; buried dead in his own garden with the ones who raised him up buried beside him. His bones were in Tennessee, but his ghost had been reported as far away as Las Vegas, Hollywood and Wichita. I wasn't one to dispute those sightings; my own mother's ghost had been to all of those places, too.

I stared up at the house and knew it for what it had become; a temple of ghosts, a shrine to the dead. Never mind its peaceful name or its rebel gates; the mansion was just another tourist trap, set out on the roadside to take in a buck.

I paid seven dollars for my ticket, but I couldn't use it right away. The tours were numbered and grouped and I had a ticket for group seven and wouldn't be seeing the inside of Elvis Presley's haunted mansion until later in the morning. I wandered up the boulevard, got stoned on a bus stop bench and killed time over an early lunch at a hamburger stand. I was splurging a lot in Memphis on things I usually wouldn't; the taxi, the Graceland tour and restaurant meals, but I decided over a greasy cheeseburger that I would rent a cheap room for the night and sleep in a bed for the first time in weeks, indulge myself with a hot shower and some

MTV. I would be nearly broke by the time I left Memphis and stocked up for the road, but I had been flat broke just three days before and I knew how to make money on the highway; there was always freight to lump or a diner hanging a HELP WANTED sign. If I was cheap about the room and careful with my wallet, I could get by on the road just fine for a while. I'd have to live slim for a week to live fat for a day, but in Memphis I stopped being a tramp and played the part of a tourist.

I tried to, at least. I had been too long on the road to make any kind of good tourist and the difference between me and all the other pilgrims out on Elvis Presley Boulevard was that I was the only one of us who didn't *want* to be there. I had hitched hundreds of miles to be there and now that I had arrived, I didn't even want to take the tour.

My mother would have gone to Graceland, if she had lived. She would have gone there or spent her life dreaming of going, but she died nearly a full month before the estate was ever opened to the public. My mother would have wept at the gates and prayed at the graves, but my mother was as dead as Elvis and she had a shrine of her own, that I kept in my heart like a dream and a curse. I had been down every road, running away from her ghost, and I'd be no different than the tourists in that trap on the hill, if I let her start leading me now.

I left the scraps of my lunch on the table and went outside for a smoke. A woman in an Elvis t-shirt and a ridiculously large pair of pink sunglasses asked me for the time and I told her I didn't wear a watch.

"Oh, dear," she said, "I'm in group six. I don't want to miss my tour."

I pointed to a clock in the burger joint's window and she sighed and waved my cigarette smoke away from her face.

"Plenty of time," she said, "I'm *so* excited, though, about seein' The King's mansion"

I shrugged, pulled my ticket from the pocket of my shirt and held it out to her.

"You wanna see it twice?"

She was suspicious and she told me so.

"You're scalpin' tickets to Graceland?" she said, "I'm sure that might be against the law."

I shook my head.

"I'm just giving it to you," I promised, "Group seven. You can go right back in as soon as you come out."

"Oh, that *would* be something."

"Yeah," I said, "Like ridin' the roller coaster twice."

She took the ticket from my hand with a hesitant smile. She asked me why I was giving her the ticket and I told her I had bought it and changed my mind about taking the tour.

"But why?" she said, "Why in the world wouldn't you take the tour."

"I got reasons," I said, "But mostly, it doesn't seem right."

She frowned.

"Well, what's *wrong* about it?"

I shrugged and I told her, even though I thought I shouldn't.

"Do you know Graceland used to be outside of town, before they built up all around it?"

She shook her head.

"I didn'*t* know that," she said, "But what's that got to do with anything about takin' the tour?

"Elvis bought that house when he got tired of people crowding around his place in town, standing outside his gate all day," I said, "It seems a little shitty; people doin' it now that he's dead, and walking right through his rooms, too."

"Well, Jesus Christ!" she said, "You don't have to ruin it for *everyone*."

I caught a bus downtown, claimed my gear from the Trailways locker and spent fourteen dollars and change for a dingy second-floor room in a lousy hotel a few blocks south of the depot. I went out once, for smokes and a bottle of soda, then I spent the day inside, smoking pot and watching music videos. In the evening, I had a shower and fell asleep stretched out on the bed before full dark.

I dreamed that night there was a knock at the door and I knew it was my mother. I rose from the bed to let her in, but when I opened the door, she wasn't there; just a swirling haze of dusty rain. I stepped out onto the walkway and leaned over the railing, dust between my toes and blowing into my eyes.

My mother stood at the curbside, leaning on the open passenger door of a long black car, and dust rose all around her like a swarm of flies. The car's engine was running; I could hear it growling impatiently while my mother stood on the sidewalk, staring up at me through the swirling grit.

"You broke our date, Richie," she hollered, "And you tried to run away."

She was wearing the same blue dress and leather jacket that I knew from another dream and an old photograph, but she wasn't young anymore. She was older in that dream than she had lived to be; old and wrinkled and her black hair had gone white.

"You tried to run away," she hollered again, "But Elvis knew where you went to and he brought me back."

I heard the dead car's engine rev and Elvis mumbled something from the driver's seat that sounded like, "You comin' or *not*, baby?"

My mother shook her head and waved the man of her dreams away.

"I'm not ready to go," she said, "My son still needs me."

The car turned to dust and was gone, a growling specter on the storm, and the wind chased me back into the room. I slammed the door behind me and swore I wouldn't answer if my mother knocked again, but she had beaten me inside and was sitting blue and dusty in a chair.

I woke up with a start, certain that I had heard myself scream, and I smoked with the lamp on and didn't turn it off for an hour. When I got back into bed, I tossed and turned beneath the sheet, but I knew I wouldn't sleep again, if I stayed in that room.

I pulled on my jacket and jeans, tossed the room key on the table and left as quietly as a thief. A few blocks away, there was a park with low trees and dark corners and I rolled out my blankets and slept.

There was someone else sleeping there, too, somewhere across the field beneath some other tree. I never saw him, but twice he cried out in his sleep and I wondered if he was dreaming of *his* mother, too.

I didn't think he saw me, either, or even knew that I had been there, but it didn't matter if he did or if he didn't. I was a stranger and a shadow everywhere I went and, in the morning, I'd be gone my way again, still going south and haunted.

PART TWO

ROADSIDE BLUES AND HYMNS

ONE
ARKANSAS RAIN

I left Memphis early in the morning, while the sky was still dark on the Tennessee line, and walked most of the day through eastern Arkansas, following the highway south into rainy grey. I was catching up to the storm, chasing it all morning and afternoon and when I finally hooked a ride in the evening, the rain was falling softly and the clouds were gaining black weight. I was damp and tired and lucky to ride out some of the storm in the warm, dry cab of a noisy Peterbilt truck.

I traded names with the driver and shrugged out of my damp jacket. I dug through my pack for a towel, pilfered from a motel, and blotted my face and hair.

"How long you been walkin' out in that rain?" the trucker said. He was a wide man with a wide smile hidden in a thick red beard.

"It only started raining on me the last hour," I said, "But I've been walkin' since Memphis."

The driver looked surprised.

"That's a long ol' way to walk," he said, "No wonder you look plumb tuckered out."

I was tired enough that I had forgotten his name, though he'd only just told it to me. The night before had been restless and I'd hardly slept, even after I fled the hotel, chased from my rented room by my mother's ghost. In the park, I slept in fits, curled up on the stony ground, still shaken by my mother's visitation.

"I feel like I walked half-way across Arkansas,"

The driver smiled and shook his head.

"Not quite so far," he said, "But you come more than thirty miles from Memphis."

We talked a little longer, with the radio playing, but the low, steady rumble of the road beneath the wheels and the low, steady mumble of his voice took on the rhythm of an old-time highway lullaby. I fell fast asleep with my head against the window, drooling down my cheek and onto the collar of my shirt all the way through Arkansas, dreaming of a dusty storm ahead and a phantom car following behind me.

I woke up suddenly, the trucker's hand on my shoulder, shaking me free of my dreams. I pressed myself against the door and slipped my hand down along my knee, an easy reach for the door-handle, or for my knife. I hadn't strapped it on my thigh that morning, just tucked it in my boot cuff and rolled the leg of my jeans down over the handle.

"Woah! Easy now, kid."

He jerked his big, rough hand away from my shoulder and smiled through his beard. He offered both hands, palms up and empty, in front of his face. There was no trouble in his sleepy eyes or on his face; just the same wide smile he had shown me earlier that night.

"Just wakin' you up, son," he said, "This is where I gotta let you off. Didn't mean to scare you none."

The truck was stopped on the shoulder of the highway, the windshield wipers squeaking back and forth and rain falling gently in its headlight's glow. I wiggled into my jacket, reached behind me for the strap of my pack and opened the door.

"Thanks for the ride, mister. Sorry I slept all the way," I said, "I wasn't scared though."

His smile opened for a soft, slow chuckle.

"Sure, you were," he said, "Ain't no shame in it. Lord knows what kind of troubles you've had out on the road."

"You caught me in a dream," I said, "That's all."

I climbed out onto the chrome step-side, one hand slinging my pack across my shoulder, the other still wrapped around the door-handle.

"Thanks again, mister."

I jumped from the truck and my bootheels sunk into the soft mud along the roadside. I reached up to push the door shut, but the driver leaned across the cab and held it open, that same honest smile hiding just beneath his beard.

"Ain't much traffic through here this time of the night and the weather is damned shitty. You wanna ride on home with me and rest up for a couple days?"

For just the briefest moment, his forehead crinkled up and his smile almost went south for a frown.

"Hell, the wife'll have me in the doghouse a little bit for it,' he said, "But she'll come around by the time I hit the road again Monday morning. I can carry you on a little further then."

I squinted up into the misty rain and then looked up at the big man whose name I had forgotten. I shook my head.

"I'm gonna keep on goin' from here," I told him, "It ain't raining all that hard."

"If you're sure about it, then..."

He tipped his trucker's cap and reached up onto the dashboard, took his wallet in his hand and pulled out two twenty-dollar bills. He handed them down to me and I took them without an argument. I was broke, and I mean flat.

On my way out of Memphis, I had stopped into a diner for breakfast; one last splurge before I got back on the road. I had walked out of the diner with just over thirty dollars left in my pocket and met an old woman on the sidewalk. She had asked me if I had any change to spare, anything at all to help her feed her husband and grandchildren.

She looked back toward a car parked in the restaurant's lot, a tired-looking old station wagon with Michigan plates and four ragged tires that reminded me of all the used cars my mother had driven when I was a boy. An old man and two small children stared at us from the wagon and the woman began to explain their hard luck, but I stopped her and pulled my thin fold of bills from my pocket. I peeled away the twenty and she took it with a tearful smile, but I felt cheap and guilty shoving the rest of the money back in my jeans.

Twenty dollars wasn't even going to feed them for the day or put gas in the station wagon. Every dollar in my pocket had come from someone who meant to help me and I had eaten for the last three days on the kindness of strangers. My belly was full and I had a pack of Pall Malls in my jacket. I had meant to buy batteries and a few cans of chili or Spam, but I traded them for a warm embrace when I tucked the last of the bills into her hand and I walked out of Memphis with just a few coins in my pocket.

I stood on the damp edge of the highway, two hundred miles south of that diner, looking up at a stranger who had handed me more than I had given away and I felt a small shame that I couldn't remember his name.

"Hey, mister! What did you say your name was?"

He tipped his cap once more.

"Name's Ron," he said, "Ronald Goddard."

I thanked him again and he pulled the door shut with a muffled thump. The big truck rumbled and huffed its way back out onto the wet blacktop and turned left down a long country road.

The rain was still light, but falling steadily, and I regretted turning down Ron's offer of a spare bed. It was the briefest of regrets, though, and I told myself that staying behind on the road was the best thing I could have done to repay the trucker for his kindness. Somewhere down that road, maybe not very far, Ronald Goddard's wife was waiting for him to come home from the road and I imagined he would get a warmer welcome if he weren't dragging some stray behind him when he got there.

I watched the bobtail tractor rock away down that thin stretch of gravel, big wheels spraying loose stones and splashes of rain, until the glow of its taillights washed out in the deepening mist. Ron gave a farewell pull on the Peterbilt's air-horn, its honking moan calling out from the gloom like a bad dream's bird. I thought of the raven cawing from a signpost back in Tennessee, but the horn sounded more like a loon, low and lonesome in the rainy dark.

I knelt on the edge of the road and dug through my pack, the rain sneaking under the collar of my jacket, slipping beneath the open neck of my shirt and lazing down my back, cool on my skin. I found a threadbare cap in the deep end of my pack, a hand-me-down from some other trucker on some other rainy night, and tugged it down tight on my head. I searched my jacket for the open box of cigarettes, shook one free and fished my lighter from my jeans. I cupped my hands around the cigarette and lit it out of the rain beneath the brim of my cap. I smoked, hunkered down on the side of a lonely road, with the rain and the trees whispering all around me in the twilight.

In the lowering dark, the woods along the highway's edge stood thick and forbidding and mysterious, like a fantasy forest in some grim fairytale. There were pines, tall and bristly, standing guard against the road and willows, too, slouched and wearing weeping robes. Beneath the taller trees, the forest was crowded with shadowy shrubs, peasant saplings and brown, begging weeds. The sound of the rain through the branches and boughs was a soft-spoken warning, the kind you only hear when you're alone and afraid in the night.

Down the highway, there was the faint glow of a lamp, struggling atop its post to find its way out of the rain. I turned my jacket's collar up against the wind and slung my pack, shoved my hands deep in my pockets and trudged up the road toward that weak, yellow glow.

A small truck blasted by, going too fast for the weather, and I hurried off the blacktop and into the mud. I hung my thumb out in the air, but the driver didn't notice and the truck never slowed. In a passing whoosh of wind and mist, it was gone into the dark and I was alone again in the Arkansas rain.

Under the highway lamp, I dug through my pack again, found the plastic bag that kept my journal and papers dry and unfolded a tattered U.S. highway map, bought at a Texaco station in 1982. It was torn at some of the creases, wrinkled at the edges and marked with notes and scribbles only I could ever read. I had carried it with me for years and the funny thing about that map was it rarely told me where I was going and it was often forgetful of where I'd been, but it always knew exactly where I was.

Well, almost always.

Figuring by the last mile-marker I'd passed and the highway sign hanging from the light-post, the map had me on a lonesome stretch numbered 278, between the small town of Camden and the even smaller town of Warren. I was on the westbound side of the highway, heading toward Camden and beyond to Interstate 30, but I had my mind set on the Mississippi River. I crossed the highway to the eastbound side and started walking back toward Warren, back in the direction I had come from.

Passing cars were few and far between, and I walked with my head down in the rain; on the roadway when I could and in the mud whenever a car came splashing up behind me. I stuck my thumb out in front of every car that passed, but the rain hadn't softened the sympathies of anyone out on that road and none of them stopped to pick me up or even slowed to check me out.

I walked along for miles, listening to the birds and bugs in the woods and the rain, falling on the blacktop and dripping through the trees. I was soaked clean through my clothes and thick mud covered my boots and clung to the bottom of my jeans. I was thirty or more miles outside of Warren, hungry and almost out of smokes, when I came upon an unlighted billboard, leaning away from the wind on the highway's edge.

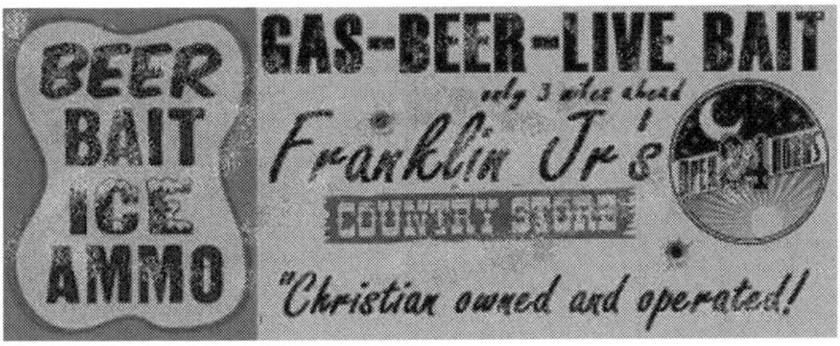

The sign was old and faded, the paint cracked and peeling, but it promised a 24-hour general store just three miles ahead and I hoped it wasn't lying. I heard the hum of a fast-moving car and its headlights splashed across the old billboard as it passed, but I didn't bother hanging my thumb out or even glancing at the driver. I slung my pack, wiped the rain from my face and walked on east, watching in the distance for the lights Franklin Jr's country store.

TWO
OPEN ALL NIGHT

The sign had told the truth and the store, dimly lit and in need of a new coat of paint, was open. There were no cars at the gas pumps or in the dirt lot, only puddles of rain and an old red bicycle propped against a front porch post. I knocked my boots against the wooden steps to get most of the mud off, left my pack on the porch and a cowbell clanged above my head when I yanked open the door.

A freckle-faced, red-headed boy about my own age looked up from a magazine and leaned slightly over the counter.

"Hey! Hello," he said. "How you doin' tonight?"

"I'm wet," I said, "Hungry, too, but mostly I'm just wet."

I walked up and down the short aisles, my muddy boots clomping on the wooden floor, rain dripping from my hair and my jacket. From a row of canned and dried goods, I took a few tins of chili and a plastic package of beef jerky, tucked them under my arm and found some batteries a few aisles over.

The kid behind the counter never took his eyes off me while I browsed, but his expression gave away more curiosity than suspicion. There was a coffee counter at the back of the store and I filled a large foam cup with thick, black ooze, tried to save it with cream and sugar, and grimaced when I tasted it.

At the front of the store, I piled my purchases on the top of a glass counter and the kid started punching buttons on the cash register. I asked him for two packs of Pall Mall and he reached above his head to pull the cigarettes from a big plastic rack.

'You ain't from 'round here, are you?" he asked, "I think I know every face in this part of the county."

"I'm passin' through," I told him, reaching in my pocket for the money Ron had given me, and the kid looked out the window at the parking lot and the fuel pumps.

"Where's your car at?" he said, "You break down out on 278? That why you're soppin' wet an' everything?"

I told him I hadn't had any car trouble, that I didn't even have a car and when I said I was hitchhiking through, his mouth dropped open in surprise. You'd have thought I told him I was travelling with a dancing elephant or Siamese twins.

"No kidding! You're hitchin'?" he said, "Well, you sure picked a time to come down through here, what with this storm an' all."

I shrugged my shoulders and said something about the rain not being too bad and he said the storm was going to get much worse before the sun came up. He nodded toward a small boombox on the shelf behind him, its speakers whispering some low-volume farm report.

"I been listening to the AM station down in Shreveport; I only get it late at night. They give the weather every hour and they say it's gonna come down *hard* tonight. That's what they're *sayin'*, at least."

Great. I'll have to find somewhere to pitch my tent.

The kid finished ringing up my items, I handed him a twenty and as he counted out my change he said, "I didn't charge you for the coffee. That stuff's been sittin' on that burner all night long."

He shrugged.

"I used to make a fresh pot every couple hours, but the ol' man put a stop to that on account of we ain't got much overnight business."

I took a bitter sip from the foam cup.

"I've had worse, believe it or not" I said, "But thanks for not makin' me pay for it."

I tucked the cigarettes inside my jacket, grabbed the small paper bag he'd shoved my food and batteries into and turned to leave.

"Hey!' he said, his face split by a goofy grin, "You wearin' an earring in your ear there?"

I touched my fingers to my left lobe and scowled. "Yeah. Why you askin' me?"

He shook his head, still grinning.

"Well, it ain't nothin' to me," he said, "I been up to Little Rock a buncha times, and we got the MTV at *my* house. You just ought to be careful 'round here is all."

He sighed through his grin.

"Some of these ol' boys might like to take you for some kinda queer or something."

"I'm not a queer...or *something*," I said.

"Nope; I didn't think you was," he told me, "You just ain't from around here, that's all. Heck, I'd give you a ride myself when I get off work in the morning, but I ain't got a car, either; just that ol' bike and I'm gonna get plenty soaked myself ridin' home."

I nodded at him and walked out under that clanging bell and as the door swung closed behind me he hollered after me offering what he probably thought was wise and friendly advice.

"Don't go takin' no rides from niggers! They'll just as soon rob you."

I sat on the porch of the country store, lit a cigarette, and sipped the shitty coffee.

It was hot, at least

THREE
A GOSPEL FLOOD

The market dimmed into the darkness behind me and the night grew thin, the way it does in the last small hours before the dawn. The rain grew bolder until the mist that had mocked me all night long became a sudden, pounding downpour. Without so much as a warning flash of lightning or a cautious roll of thunder, the storm lowered down right over me and opened wide. I was already wet straight through to my skin, but I was taking on water and the low, dark Arkansas sky threatened to drown me in my boots, right there on the broken white spine of U.S. Route 278.

I had to get out of the storm and find a place to shelter and get my wet clothes off my back. I stood in the middle of the road and let my pack, heavier now with the rain, slump from my shoulder to the ground. I peered into the woods on both sides of the highway, tried to see beyond the curtain of rain that shrouded the trees, but it was a forest of shadow and shade and I was a boy of broad imagination.

I'd been caught out in the rain on a hundred lonely highways and made my bed beneath the branches of ten thousand darkened trees, but I didn't trust that road, so slick and shiny in the darkness. I didn't trust the trees, either; the way they crept right up to the blacktop and crouched there quietly. It sounded like a forest full of secrets a forest that knew how to keep them, and the shiny ribbon of highway that slithered through it hissed like a black snake in the rain. It felt like the kind of road that doesn't wear down the soles of your boots; it just eats them.

I looked over my shoulder, back toward the general store, but it was so far out of sight it might never have been there at all. The rain was so heavy and noisy that I couldn't hear my boots thumping against the asphalt and I could hardly see my way ahead through the darkness.

The road was flooded, but I could still see the white center line and I followed it through the night until I saw the vague shape of a sign on the highway's murky edge.

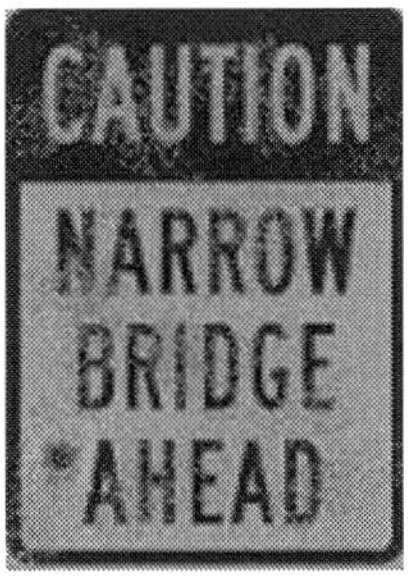

I shrugged my pack up higher on my back, bent my head against the rain and hurried up the highway following the rising sound of a rushing, swollen stream. My boots splashed hard on the flooded blacktop then softly in muddy weeds as I came upon the bridge and slid down a loose, steep embankment to the edge of the creek. I tumbled into the shadows at the edge of the bridge's cellar, wiped the rain from my eyes, and when I saw a small fire, flickering in the concrete cave, I was already standing exposed in its glow.

The sign out on the roadside had warned me that the bridge was narrow, but it hadn't said anything about the troll that lurked beneath it.

It hunched beside the fire, a dark silhouette as vague and brooding as the shadow it cast against the cracked, slimy bones of the bridge. Its face was greasy and dim in the fire's weak light and its milky eyes fell upon me like dead lanterns.

Something dark and wet trickled from one corner of its mouth and it held something long and jagged in its claws. I could smell its sour sweat from six feet away.

I stood still and silent until my eyes were no longer charmed by the swirling shadows and firelight and, of course, the beast beneath the bridge wasn't a troll at all; Just a large, ugly man with a broken bottle clasped between his fat hands.

He leaned over the campfire and its glow revealed the whole of his unfortunate ugliness. He blinked then stared into my face, a slippery grin spreading thin across his own.

"Murderer or milkman?"

Huh?

I let my pack fall to the ground and I wished my knife had been strapped to my belt instead of tucked down the cuff of my boot. My first thought had been to turn and flee, to leave him behind in the dripping shelter of the bridge and let the storm rinse away the sight and the scent of him, but my pack was heavy and the embankment I'd come down was slick. If I ran and he was the type to chase me, he'd have me by my ankles before I reached the road, so I stood in the light of his fire, stared straight back into his rheumy gaze and summoned the kind of frightened courage that only comes from circumstance.

"*Well*?"

His voice was raspy and low.

"Murderer or milkman?"

I shrugged and my eyes slid from his greasy face to his snakeskin belt and all the way down to his worn and weathered boots. If he had a knife, it was tucked out of sight, but he was a very big man and he had that jagged bottle in his hands. Our eyes crossed paths again and his grin didn't falter.

"I don't know what that means," I told him.

He tipped the bottle to his mouth, pulled a sloppy swig from its broken neck and breathed a sigh of invisible fire. He wiped the back of his hand across his lips and it came away bloodied.

"Well, when I was a kid...just a little bitty one," he said, "My grandmama used to say that a body out creepin' about in the twilight hours is either a murderer or a milkman."

He took another long pull from the bottle and settled back against the bridge's belly, his face cast in shadow, his voice a graveyard whisper.

"So, which one are *you*, boy?"

I almost told him I was neither, but instead I spoke out a memory,

"*My* gramma used to tell *me* that if I couldn't wake her up in the morning, it meant she'd died in her sleep."

In the fiery shadows, The Troll-Man slapped his knee and laughed. No; he giggled.

"Oh, I *like* that!" he said, "I like that one *a lot*!"

He leaned closer to the fire's glow and his grin spread like a plague across his face, bulging his cheeks and poisoning his eyes with wicked delight.

"Did that happen?" he nearly whispered, "Did you find grandma dead in her bed one morning? I bet you pissed your pee-jays, for sure."

"No," I told him, hunkering down, "She died wide awake and she was looking at me. That ain't so funny though, is it?"

My fingers hung loose at my ankle, so nervous, so sure and so close to my knife and he shut his giggle up behind a slanted smile.

"Well, now, we're gettin' ourselves off to a heavy start, ain't we?"

He tipped the bottle back again then tilted it out in front of him, an offer of welcome and peace.

"You come down under here to get outta the rain," he said, "So, don't just stand out there *in* it."

The fire hissed and crackled. Red hot embers drifted free above the flames, but burned out fast and left pale ashes in the air.

"C'mon, now...I ain't no murderer. Ain't no *milkman*, neither."

FOUR
BLOOD AND MOONSHINE

I chose shelter over the storm, the fire over the rain, ducked my head under the bridge's edge and dragged my pack into the shadows. I sat down hard on a crumbling slab of dusty concrete and the stranger tossed a fat length of dry pine-branch onto the crackling fire between us.

"To foul weather and fair friends," he said, pulling another swallow from the bottle, "Or *fair* weather and *foul* friends. Don't make no never mind to me."

Let's see which kind you are.

I watched him through the fire's thin smoke, a ragged man who spoke in riddles that sounded like veiled threats. I was reminded of Bilbo Baggins' encounter with the wretched Gollum in the caverns beneath Goblin Town and I wished I had a magic ring of my own to hide me from his watery eyes.

The dark trickle I'd seen at the corner of his mouth was blood. It ran from his lip to the bottom of his chin and there were dark spots and splotches where it had dripped onto his shirt.

His hair was long and tangled, his clothes were baggy and filthy and his skin was so greasy that it shined in the firelight. His fingernails were long and dirty, yellow claws with black tips and his eyes were deathly and wet.

His boots, two beat-down lumps of old leather with frayed laces, dried beside the fire and his feet, wrapped in tattered socks too thin to hold in all his toes, rested on the loose ring of hot stones that surrounded the flames.

"Your lip is bleeding," I told him.

"Yeah...ain't it?"

He wiped his hand absently across his chin.

"I broke my bottle," he said, "Tripped on my *own* feet comin' down here and broke it, but that ain't any excuse to go and waste what weren't spilt."

He tilted the bottle toward me for the second time and I took it from his hands and held it beneath my nose. It smelled sweet, sour and *flammable*, like kerosene laced with sugar to fool you into thinking it wouldn't kill you.

I raised the bottle to the fire's glow and shook it, peering through the dark glass. The liquid inside was the color of honey, at least in that strange light, and a few bits of broken glass swirled at the bottom, shining like tiny diamonds in the dark.

"What is this stuff?" I said.

The Troll-Man smiled and whistled through his teeth. They were yellow, shiny and slick.

"Boy, that's corn liquor," he told me, "Finest distillation in three counties."

"It's moonshine." I said, "Is that what it is? Moonshine?"

"Moon shines, yes it does," he said, "But so does a monkey's ass."

He giggled and slapped his knee, nodded his head at the bottle in my hands.

"Have a slug, kid. It'll warm you up for sure. Hell, *two* slugs and your shirt is like to dry right there on your back."

I wiped the snaggle-toothed neck of the bottle on my sleeve, put it carefully to my lips and tipped it back. My mouth flooded with homemade fire and it went down my throat hot and sneaky. I squeezed my eyes closed and gasped and for just a moment, as the heat spread in my chest and through my belly, I thought the rainwater that soaked my shirt would turn to steam and prove The Troll-Man's drunken claim to be a fact.

"*Jeez*!" I hissed, "That's poison."

It did taste like poison, and I had never liked drinking, but the slight, sudden fuzziness in my fingertips and my tongue was comforting and the warmth in my belly made me feel miles away from the rain that lashed at the edges of the bridge and flooded the bottom of the gulley. I tipped the bottle again and drank.

That second shot went down a little smoother than the first, but not so much that I didn't sputter and cough as that fuzzy fire spread from my belly to my blood.

The stranger held out his hand and I passed the bottle back across the fire. He took another throaty swig of the whiskey and coughed a mess of phlegm into the dirt.

"You got any tobacco, boy?" he asked me, "I bet you do. You look like a fella who smokes."

I slipped my hand inside my jacket and pulled out my smokes. The box was damp, but the cigarettes inside it were dry and I shook a pair of them loose, passed one to my foul weather friend and poked the other between my lips. I struck my lighter in the dim and put it to my cigarette and he stuck the tip of his against the smoldering red end of a stick on the campfire.

He sat back against the embankment, twisted the filter off the cigarette and drew on it so hard that his cheeks puckered in. He stared cross-eyed at the glowing orange tip and snorted thick smoke out through his nose.

"Tailor-mades," he said. "I mostly roll my own, but beggars can't be choosers."

We sheltered together in the handmade cavern beneath the bridge, smoking my cigarettes and drinking his liquor, and the rain blew in occasionally to whisper down my neck, a chill reminder that I was trapped here, not invited.

I only had four small pulls from The Troll-Man's bottle, but the liquor was stronger than anything I had ever drank before. It was sneaky, too, and it crept through my blood like a sudden sickness.

Don't get drunk. Don't fall asleep. The rain sounds just like a train.

Those were clouded thoughts, a late warning to myself as the bottle grew heavy in my hand. My eyes lowered until I could only keep one open at a time, then neither of them, and I fell hard into the sleep of the dead, the slumber of drunks.

I dreamed long silver tracks and a long, black train. Its wheels hissed on the rails and black smoke stretched out behind it like a phantom noose and The Troll-Man leaned out of the big steam locomotive, waving a ratty engineer's cap in the air, shouting.

"I *like* that! I like that one *a lot*!"

I can't get up...can't get up...I can't get up...

I couldn't move. I was stretched across cold railroad tracks, but no ropes held me bound; just the weight of a hulking shadow pressing me against the rails, smothering my escape, and then the train was fast upon me and it crushed my throat.

Wake up, wake up, wake up...

I awoke to the roar of the train (*no, it's rain*) and The Troll-Man was on me like three-hundred pounds of soft death. His fat legs straddled me like a vice and his face hung over mine, near and leering, His mouth was open and the tip of his earthworm tongue waggled back and forth between his shiny teeth.

He had one giant hand clasped around my throat and the other fumbled with the buckle of my belt. His breath was corn liquor and cancer, his sweat was greasy rain on my face and the small, hardened knot in his trousers was a threatening, begging disgrace.

My head felt dull and thick, I could taste the whiskey on my own tongue and I could barely breathe with his fingers clawing into my throat. He wasn't strong, just heavy, and I couldn't slip out from beneath him. His wide ass was dead weight on my legs, but my arms were free.

I couldn't reach my knife, but I loosened his grip on my throat with one hand, made a fist of the other and beat on the side of his head.

I drew in a deep gasp of air as his hand let loose of my neck, but he planted his palm on my cheek and pressed his thumb into my eye, twisted my face against the dirt.

"C'mon, now," he said, his voice a rattling hiss, "This ain't got to go the hard way. Just lemme get it in my mouth."

He pressed harder on my face, his thumb dug deeper into the corner of my eye and the fingers of his other hand worked through my belt and my zipper and wiggled wickedly under my jeans.

I had one eye squeezed shut, about to burst beneath his thumb and the other wide open against the ground and in the flickering light of the fire I saw the broken bottle tipped over in the dirt, its jagged mouth like a copperhead's fangs.

I stretched my hand across the damp ground, grabbed the bottle where it was thick and round and slashed the air, then his face, with the mean, jagged edge. Twin gashes opened up beneath his eye, parting the flesh of his cheek, and blood, red, but black in the dark, oozed from his face and dripped warm onto mine.

He roared in pain and reared back from the swinging bottle. The hand he'd planted on my face flew up to his own, the one he had jammed down my pants retreated and I stuck the broken bottle like a blade into his soft, fleshy chest. It didn't sink in deep, but it was sharp, and he howled and tumbled backward, rolling in the dirt, clutching his bloody face.

"You dirty mother-humper!" he shouted, "You Goddamned mother-humper!"

I got to my feet with my knife in my hand, the blade long and gleaming and thick, and I kicked him hard in the ribs, once then twice. Bone cracked beneath the steel tips of my boot. He snarled and writhed in the damp moss and dirt and I turned, grabbed my pack up and fled; out of the shadows of the bridge into the last dark patch of night, splashing down the gulley in the rain with my belt hanging loose and my zipper wide open.

I climbed up from the creek-side at a place where the embankment cut low and the roots of a big, twisted tree reached out over the water. I ran across the highway, lost my footing for a moment in the mud, and burst blindly into the forest I'd avoided all night long.

I rushed through the trees, squeezed under a barbed-wire fence and snuck across a pasture where cows slept in the shelter of a long, wooden shack. There was a darkened house in the distance, where I might have gone for help, but I thought of risking a shotgun in some sleepy farmer's hands and ran for the dark of the forest instead.

I huddled against the trunk of a willow and hid beneath its hanging branches as the cows lowed out in the pasture and the moon moved across the sky, a faded lamp behind the clouds. The rain stopped at dawn, scolded by the sun, and I slept soaking wet in a shroud of low morning fog.

FIVE
A MURDER OF CROWS

When I woke up, the fog had lifted and the mid-morning sunlight streamed through the trees to warm damp patches of the forest floor. The cows were awake in their pasture beyond the trees and they bawled and grunted as they grazed. I could hear the sounds of cars and trucks rumbling past on the highway.

My throat was bruised and my left eye was swollen, bloodshot and blurred. I was lucky The Troll-Man hadn't popped it out of my head with his thumb. I had red scratches across my belly where The Troll-Man's grimy fingers had clawed at my jeans and I hoped they weren't infected with the filth from under his nails.

I pushed my hair back out of my eyes and dug for my cigarettes. The pack I'd opened the night before was gone, left and lost beneath The Troll-Man's bridge, and I smacked the fresh box against the palm of my hand several times, tore the cellophane off and smoked with my head resting against the willow tree's damp trunk.

I wanted coffee, but all the brush and branches around me were still wet from the rain so I didn't bother with a fire that wouldn't burn. I ate chili cold from the can and gnawed on a fat strip of jerky while I dug through my pack for a dry change of clothes.

The rain had found its way deep into my big duffle and most of my clothes were wet, but I managed a pair of socks and some jeans that were only damp, changed out of the wet ones I had slept in and hung my shirt from a tree branch to dry.

I lazed in the warmth of the sun and got stoned, with fresh batteries in my Walkman and Springsteen confessing to murder in my ears. I thought about my spooky chance meeting with The Troll-Man the night before and about the tricky way the light of the day made my narrow escape seem like something from a dream long ago.

Time could be slippery on the road, but I knew that I'd come close to being killed only hours before. The marks on my throat were fresh and raw and the sunlight was a rod of white fire in my wounded eye.

I wondered how near or far The Troll-Man was. He could have been gone, miles down the road, or still hiding under his bridge. He might have been nearer than that, lurking in the woods, watching and waiting for me.

A shadow passed in front of the sun and I flinched. I reached between my blankets for my knife, thinking that The Troll-Man had somehow crept silently upon me, but there was nobody there in the woods, just a sudden cackling and cawing and a chill that crawled up my spine and onto the breeze.

Above me, the sky filled with birds, their deathly black wings raging against the vicious blue. They flew low overhead, just above the trees, spread out across the sky like a heckling band of dark angels, but it was only an eastbound flock of loud-mouthed crows.

Murder. They're called a murder, not a flock.

I must have read that in a book or learned it from a movie, but I couldn't remember which one and it didn't even matter. In that moment, I knew what it meant and I hid in the willow's lap from the cackling cries and sharp eyes of the crows.

They seemed like searchers, calling out across the countryside, seeking something or someone and I wondered if they were looking for Lonnie James, to see if his cancer had killed him yet. They passed me over as one of the living and cawed away east in a hurry. Maybe they'd grown impatient for Lonnie to die and decided to find him and kill him.

I would be going east, too, but not before the last straggling spies had fluttered overhead and caught up to the flock.

I strapped my knife to my hip, but left my shirt untucked to keep it a secret. I shouldered my wet pack and walked through the trees toward the sounds of the occasional car blowing by out on the highway. I avoided the pasture now that it was light out and stuck to the tree-line where no one could see me from the windows of the farmhouse across the field.

Back out on 278, I started walking east, but I looked back twice at the narrow bridge a half mile behind me and foolish curiosity got the better of me.

I stashed my pack in a clump of bushes along the roadside and crept to the bridge, cautiously, under cover of the trees. I snuck along the flooded gulley, ducked behind the limbs of a crooked tree and peered into the daytime shadows beneath the bridge. I tugged the hem of my shirt up over my knife, and listened.

All I heard were the birds and the breeze, not a car on the road or a sound from the shadows. I ducked under the bridge and stood beside the dead fire's cold ashes.

The Troll-Man was gone.

The broken bottle lay discarded, a dead snake with dried blood on its fangs, and there were big drops of blood on the concrete slab where I'd wrestled the stranger and won.

I found my lost pack of cigarettes on the ground, with seven left inside, and smiled as I tucked it in my shirt pocket. The bridge rumbled and shook as a big truck rushed overhead, startling me, and I left the darkened cavern and climbed back up to the sun and the highway.

I walked with my thumb hanging out and the day stretched lean and warm, but the road still felt like a bad one and the sun didn't pierce the dread, gloomy mood of the forest.

I came upon a great black bird, pecking at the putrid flesh of a dead skunk in the eastbound lane of the road and thought it might have been a straggler from the flock, left behind to spy on me. It screamed at me and strutted around the road-kill as I passed, but it didn't fly away in fear.

I picked up a rock from the roadside, chucked it at the bird, and it fluttered its wings and rose up in a crooked circle, then settled back down to the road and the feast.

Lucky fuckin' bird. Last time I threw a rock, I killed something.

In the early afternoon, I caught a ride with a quiet man in a flatbed truck, loaded with hay bales and big brass pipes. We didn't talk much as we rode along together, but it wasn't an uncomfortable quiet, and the warm breeze through the open windows and the country music on the radio more than made up for all the talking we didn't do.

He took me as far as the county seat in Monticello and dropped me at a busy junction with a handshake and a smile.

"You know, that's an odd thing to see around here," he said, "A fella with an earring."

I smiled, too, and said, "So I've heard; but *some* things are odder."

I slung my pack, but he didn't pull away.

"I been tryin' not to ask," he said, "But what the *hell* happened to your face?"

"Got in a fight with a troll."

He shrugged and steered his truck back out on the road and I sat on my pack, leaned against a road sign and flashed my thumb at every passing car. Monticello was a smallish city, but it *was* the county seat and there was a fair amount of traffic at the junction, where I could catch a ride heading east or even south. I wasn't particular about the direction; I'd find the Mississippi either way I went.

SIX

SNEAKS AND SQUEAKS

I sat stranded at the junction for hours, into the late afternoon. A red Camaro slowed down and I thought I had hooked a ride, but a teenage boy in the passenger's seat hollered out at me as they crawled by.

"Get a job, *faggot*!"

He lobbed a big foam cup out the window and it splattered in the dirt at my feet, spilling ice and spraying cola on my boots. They drove off down the highway, whooping and hollering, reassured of their southern-bred masculinity, and I thought of the red-headed clerk back at Franklin's country market.

Some of these ol' boys might like to take you for some kinda queer or something.

I pulled my harmonica from my pocket and played what I knew, bits of songs, spare riffs and the train sound I'd learned in Nashville. A big Lincoln town car pulled off of the road and a skinny old black man wearing sunglasses and a string tie threw open the passenger door, smiled and hollered at me.

"Well, come on then and get yer ride, bluesman."

I was reminded a second time of the kid from the general store.

Don't take no rides from niggers.

I heaved my pack into the back seat and climbed in the front beside the grey-haired man wrapped in Ray-Ban shades. He offered his big, wrinkled hand and his long bony fingers wrapped around mine for a strong handshake. He wheeled the Lincoln back out on the junction, took the highway pushing south and lit a sweet, tangy-smelling cigar.

"Name's Stanley," he said, puffing thick smoke out the corner of his mouth, "Stanley Calvin Thomas my momma named me, but most folks call me Sneaks."

He tapped the cigar out the window and sent grey ashes on the wind.

"How 'bout you? What they call you, travelin' man?"

"Just Rick," I told him. "Thanks for the ride, mister."

"Well, now, Rick...you call me Sneaks, like everybody else does. No more o' that 'mister' stuff."

He pushed his sunglasses up on his forehead and smiled, all crinkly brown eyes and perfect white teeth.

"I seen you puffin' on that harp back there on the roadside and I says, Sneaks, you can't leave a bluesman out on the highway, no matter *how* white he might look."

We laughed and I lit a cigarette and joined him blowing smoke and tapping ashes out the windows.

"I'm no bluesman," I confessed, "I just mess around a little; try to teach myself when I'm bored."

Sneaks shifted the big cigar from one side of his grin to the other and said, "Well, c'mon, then...let's hear whatcha got."

"Oh, no sir!" I protested, "Really, I'm not any good at all."

He lowered his shades back over his eyes and grinned.

"Son, everybody who's good at anything started out bein' not very good at all," he said, "Besides, nobody rides for free, so let's hear how you blow that thing."

I took the harmonica out of my shirt pocket, turned it over so I had the right side up and put it to my lips. I played for a couple of minutes, clumsily blowing through those spare riffs and odd bits of tunes, and Sneaks slapped his flat palm against his thigh and bobbed his head while my harmonica honked and moaned.

I ran out of things to play, stopped the train on a sudden toot and slipped the harp back in my pocket.

"Well, you was right," Sneaks laughed, "You ain't very good at *all*. No, sir...no, sir."

"Well, thanks a *lot*, Sneaks."

"Well, you ain't godawful, now," he said, "You got the *idea*, you just ain't got the *feel*."

"But how's it supposed to feel?" I asked him.

His forehead wrinkled and he looked thoughtful, even with the dark glasses hiding his eyes, and when he answered, he kept a straight face, not the hint of a smile.

"Son...playin' the blues harp is *just* like kissin' a woman's hoo-ha."

I blushed.

"Um...what?"

"*Pussy*!" he laughed. "It's just like kissin' pussy."

He tapped his chest, just over his heart.

"That's the gospel truth, boy."

I laughed. "You're outta your mind, ain't you, Sneaks?"

"*I'm* outta *my* mind?"

He lifted his Ray-Bans again and looked at me crooked.

"Now, you done kissed a lotta hoo-has, youngster?"

I almost kept a straight face myself, almost looked him in the eye and almost didn't mumble.

"Well...no, not that many."

He cupped his hand around his ear and leaned toward me.

"Say *what* now? I didn't quite hear you, bluesman. What's that you said?"

I repeated my admission and he smiled big and bright and shook his head.

"That's what I thought you said. Not *many*!"

He fixed me with a solemn frown, but there was good humor in his voice.

"The white boy ain't kissed much pussy and I could tell *that* by the way he blows his harp, and he's gonna ask *me* am I outta my mind? Aw, no...no, sir."

I pulled the harmonica out of my pocket and held it out to Sneaks and he laughed so hard at my dare that he nearly howled.

"First thing, son, is you don't *ever* let another man put his mouth on your harp. *That's* how it's like pussy."

He settled back against the big seat and lazed the car up the road with one scrawny wrist resting on the steering wheel.

"You listen to ol' Sneaks now, son," he said through his smoke and his smile, "First thing you ought do with that harp is you gotta get her wet. You popped that thing in your mouth just as dry as a sawdust sammich!"

He ran his tongue over his lips like a man who's just eaten something sweet and sticky.

"You gotta lick your lips, get 'em moist like...so's they glides. The other thing is, you gotta learn how to work it."

I cocked an eyebrow at him and grinned.

"Work it," I said, "Yes, sir."

He winked and let me get away with my sarcasm.

"That's *right*. You gotta use your lips and your tongue and even your teeth, sometimes all together and sometimes one at a time. Any fool can blow on her and make her honk an' squeak, but you gotta work it to make her sing an' squeal. And that goes for blues harps and women, *too*."

I licked my lips, slid the harmonica between them and blew out a long, high whistle and Sneaks stuck a finger in his ear and twirled it around comically.

"Don't worry, boy," he grinned, "You'll get yer fair share o' practice, I'm sure."

"You think so?"

"Oh, yes, sir...yes, sir, I do!" he said and winked, "Hell, you might even kiss you some hoo-ha someday, too."

Sneaks steered the big Lincoln down 425, popped a blues cassette into the tape-deck and asked me about the bruises on my neck and under my swollen eye.

"Got in a fight," I said, "Had a little trouble back up the road last night."

He whistled through his teeth.

"Musta been a hell of a fight," he said, "Got yerself strangled from the looks o' them welts on your neck. What happened? Was it black boys?"

I touched the bruises on my throat. It hurt but the pain in my eye was worse and my vision was still blurred.

"Tell you what...I'll tell you what happened, but you gotta tell *me* something first."

"You kiddin' me, boy?" he laughed, "I done already told you the secret to blowin' blues harmonica. And kissin' pussy, too!"

"Yeah, well, I wanna know how come everybody calls you Sneaks."

He chuckled and told me a story.

When he was a boy, he and his four brothers each had two pair of shoes; sneakers for school, work and play and a shiny pair of dress shoes for church meetings and funerals and such.

I thought of the young man who had run over Huck with his car, remembered the dust on his fancy black shoes.

"We called our Sunday shoes *squeakers* 'cause of how they squeaked on the wooden church-house floor and 'cause before we ever put 'em on, momma would make sure we scrubbed up squeaky clean."

He told me that he always refused to wear his squeakers and was always arguing with his mom and getting in trouble with his old man for wearing his sneakers to church on Sunday mornings.

"The other kids started callin' me Sneakers, then just Sneaks, and most folks caught on and stuck right with it."

I looked over at him, casually classy, wearing a crisp white shirt and black cotton. Sure enough, he was wearing a pair of Converse high-top sneakers.

"That's a good story," I said. "It's a good thing you didn't like your church shoes and hate your sneakers. Everybody'd be callin' you *Squeaks*."

He laughed.

"I like that," he said, "Yes, sir, I like that *a lot*."

I flinched and thought of The Troll-Man and told Sneaks about the storm, the bridge and how I fell asleep on corn liquor and woke up with the filthy stranger trying to choke me at both ends. I told him about the fight and the broken bottle and how I escaped into the woods and hid until the morning.

"Hoo weee!" he said, "You really cut him, did you?"

I looked straight back.

"Yeah...I really did," I said, "With his own fuckin' bottle."

"Boy, you might make a bluesman one o' these days yet."

I laughed.

"Oh yeah? How many men you gotta cut to be a bluesman, Sneaks?"

He stroked his chin and grinned.

"Depends, boy. For black folks, it's just one, but a honky kid from up north...well, he's gotta stab at least a dozen fellas. And learn how to kiss a girly's hoo-ha.

SEVEN
BEANS AND BACK PORCH BLUES

He invited me to his home, offered me a shower and a couch and a washing machine and said I hadn't been to Arkansas if I hadn't had a taste of his Millie's red beans and rice. I thought of what The Troll-Man had said about fair weather and foul friends and Sneaks must have seen something in my expression,

"Ain't no harm or trouble gonna come to you under my roof, son. I'll put my skin on that."

On the outskirts of a small town, Sneaks pulled the car off the highway and we bumped down a dirt road through a neighborhood of small wooden houses, some with leaning roofs and comfortable porches, others with peeling paint and pretty potted flowers on the steps. We turned into a narrow, unpaved street where a group of boys were standing along the curb, smoking and laughing and listening to music on a big silver boom-box. They were all close to my own age, some shirtless, some with dark glasses or tattoos, all of them black. As we passed, I saw them sneering and staring, heard them muttering to each other and slinging remarks at me.

"You just mind yer own and don't be stupid and say nothin' back," Sneaks winked, "We ain't quite under my roof just yet, bluesman."

He steered the car into a dirt dooryard, got out and closed a noisy chain-link gate and brought me up on the porch and into his house. It was nicer inside than it was on the outside and it reminded me of some of the apartments in the old neighborhood where I'd grown up; the way it felt homey and clean even though it wasn't much more than a big shack.

We stood in the hallway, just inside the door, and Sneaks took off his Converse high-tops and a woman appeared down the hall with a savory, spicy breeze at her back. She stopped with her head cocked, staring at me and her eyes were surprised but not unpleasant and she said only one word.

"Oh!"

Sneaks turned and saw her. His smile broadened and beamed, his arms spread instinctively open and he went to her and hugged her close and kissed her on her smooth cheek.

She was pretty and plump and her skin was the color of caramel, a raving beauty even in her sixties. She kissed her husband and smiled at me when she let him go.

"Well, then..." she said, "Who's this beat-up lookin' white boy standin' in my front hall with his muddy boots on."

Sneaks hooted and tossed me a sparkling wink.

"Oh, boy…you startin' off on both the wrong feet with Millie."

I muttered a shy apology and kicked off my boots and Millie Thomas held out her beautiful hand and led me down the hall.

"You come on in here now and have yourself somethin' to eat," she said, "Lord knows, you look skinny enough to die."

"Don't he though?" Sneaks said, "Come on in the kitchen, son. Millie, this here fella is Rick, from way up north via destinations unknown. He's a travelin' man and an apprentice hoo-ha kisser."

Millie slapped him softly on his chest.

"Now, Stanley Thomas!" she scolded him, "Don't you be talkin' that smut in front of this boy."

"Oh, don't you worry 'bout him now, Millie," Sneaks said, "He's a *bluesman*!"

From a great iron pot, Millie ladled steaming red beans and thick broth over rice and brought it to us in big bowls with cornbread and buttermilk. I'd never drank buttermilk before and I grimaced when I took my first swallow, but when I crumbled my cornbread into it and ate the mash with a spoon, the way Sneaks and Millie did, it was delicious; the perfect remedy for the sting the spicy beans had left on my tongue.

At the table, Sneaks managed most of the talking, much to my amusement and his wife's loving reproach, and Millie asked me where I was from, but nothing else. After dinner, she showed me to the shower and gave me a thick, soft towel and a pair of striped pajamas and insisted on washing my clothes. She wouldn't hear of me doing them myself.

"Ain't nobody uses my new machine but *me*," I heard her say as she walked down the hall and left me to hot water and rich scented soap.

I indulged in the shower, lathered my skin and hair thickly and stayed in too long, jolting for a moment when Millie started the wash machine down the hall, stealing the hot water away from me. I toweled myself dry, swept back my hair, put on the slightly too-big pajamas and walked barefoot down the hall.

There was a lamp on in a comfortable sitting room and I leaned in the open doorway.

Millie was sitting in a big, cushiony chair, watching television, and she looked up at me with a smile as sweet as a kiss.

"Well, you're cleaner," she said, "But you still look beat up awful. Stanley's out on the back porch, smokin' his cigar. Go on out and have a sit with him, son."

The screen door drew closed behind me and I found Sneaks rocking smoothly in an old wooden chair, a thick cigar jammed in the corner of his lips. He was strumming a bluesy riff on a shining guitar and humming a wordless tune over the top of it.

He looked up at me as I leaned against the porch railing, a devil twinkled in his eyes and he started to sing.

Met a boy down south
On the road in Arkansas
I met a white boy way down south
He's too young to be away
From his ma
Look like he had a mean ol'
Hound dog for a pa
Got a beat-up eye
He ate my rice an' beans
He got a beat-up eye
An' he ate all of my rice an' beans
An' Lawd, you know his
Dirty ol' blue jeans
Is spinnin' round an' round
In my Millie's brand new
Washin' machine

I clapped my hands and laughed and Sneaks rocked back in his chair and drew sweet smoke from his cigar, laughing and clapping his own hands, too.

"I thought you said everybody called you Sneaks," I teased, "Miss Millie sure doesn't."

His eyes flashed softly.

"Oh, not my Millie," he admitted, "That fine woman; she can call me whatever she damn well pleases."

His laughter trickled down to a thin smile and he rested his hands on the guitar.

"Sit down an' relax, son," he said, "I'm an old man, but I ain't ever been more than three hundred miles from right here where I was born."

He looked out across the street and over the rooftops at the clear night sky.

"Tell an old boy a story and don't leave out the part about what a skinny white kid like you is doin' out on the road alone, blowin' wherever he blows and goin' where nobody knows."

I sat with him on the porch in the dark and we smoked and I told him where I'd come from and why I had left there. I hadn't expected to, but I cried almost from the start, talking about my childhood and my mother's death. I spoke quietly, just above a whisper, about strange places I had been to and the strangers I had known.

"I met a girl who said she was an angel."

"Was she one?" Sneaks said.

"I dunno," I told him, "She killed herself...to prove it, I think."

"Did she?"

I glanced at him, confused.

"Did she what?" I said, "Kill herself?

Sneaks shook his head slowly, sadly.

"Nah, you already said she did that," he said, "I meant; did she prove it 'bout bein' an angel?"

"Not to me, she didn't," I said, "But one way or another, I guess she found out for herself."

There were better things to tell about the road and Sneaks leaned forward eagerly when I told him about the traveling carnival. He closed his eyes and sighed when I described the California desert and the giant trees in the Pacific northwest.

I told him about the people: all the truckers, hippies and cowboys out on the road and I ran out of stories when I confessed that I had been to Graceland, but not gone inside.

"And here I am," I said, "And tomorrow, I'll be gone."

He smiled, but it was wistful.

"You might not be a bluesman," he sighed, "But you sure got yerself a bad mess o' blues."

"Yeah, I guess I do," I whispered, "But I don't know what to do about *that*."

"Son, I reckon you're doin' what a lotta men do when they're sufferin' the blues."

"What's that, Sneaks?" I said, "What *am* I doin' with my blues?"

"Why, you're walkin' 'em off, son. You're just walkin' 'em right off."

We sat on the porch as the evening descended and the stars winked on in the sky one by one. Sneaks picked and strummed his guitar absently and he told me stories about his life, growing up and growing old in Drew County, Arkansas.

He told me about his first job, his first car and his first love and said, "I only ever held on to *one* of them things all my life and she's settin' right inside this ol' house even now."

An old woman came shuffling along the dirt alleyway in back of the house, stopped at the gate and leaned over.

"Evenin' to you, Sneaks," she called out curiously.

Sneaks waved and called back to her

"It is a *fine* one ain't it, Etta Simms? You have yourself a real nice walk, now."

Etta Simms removed her spectacles and peered at us from across the dooryard.

"Got comp'ny, I see," she said, "Sneaks, is that a *white boy* you got up on your porch?"

"Why, yes indeed, Etta! He's a white boy, for sure."

He smiled and winked at me and called out again to Etta Simms.

"This here's my long-lost son from New York City!"

The old lady cackled and waved her hand at Sneaks.

"You ain't never been up to *New York City*."

Sneaks puffed on his cigar and said, "I sure have been up that way...once back about, oh, twenty year ago or so."

That exasperated Etta Simms and she squinted at Sneaks, and at me, too.

"You meanin' to tell me that you went up to New York City and had yourself a white woman and she had *your* baby and that boy come out *white*, without no nappy hair?"

"Why, yes ma'am, I do mean to tell you just exactly that" Sneaks grinned, "His momma was a *very* white woman, you see."

Sneaks got up from his chair and I followed him into the house and left Etta Simms shaking her head at the gate.

Inside the doorway, Sneaks clasped my hand in his and wished me a good sleep.

"What all them folks out on that road tell a stranger?" he said, "What they talk to you about?"

"You'd be surprised," I said, "Around here, everybody's been buggin' me about God; until now, I mean."

Sneaks winked.

"Don't you worry none," he said quietly, "That's comin'."

Sneaks went down the hall to his bed and Millie made the couch up with a sheet, a thin blanket and a big pillow. She fluffed the pillow between her hands like she was kneading feathery dough.

"This ol' sofa's got a middle like a swayback mule and she's hard at both ends," she said, "But you don't look so used to sleepin' in tall comfort."

I smiled at the way she said 'tall comfort'. I liked the way she and Sneaks talked. Their southern-fried drawl sounded comfortable and peaceful, not ignorant and slow like the kid at the general store or spooky and slick like The Troll-Man. They used words out of context that, once you heard them, seemed to make better sense than the word you had been expecting in its place. Sneaks had a sooty voice like smoke and bourbon and Millie's was cream and clover honey and you only had to hear them speak to know that they were both great singers.

"No, ma'am," I said, "I don't sleep much in tall comfort...or the short kind either."

She laughed and winked.

"You sleep good now, young fella. We get up at the bust o' dawn around here most days, but tomorrow bein' Sunday, I ain't fryin' no eggs until at least seven o'clock. Seven-thirty if that old man don't start hummin' while he's shavin' his scruff."

I settled into the sofa and Millie turned to leave the room and I stopped her at the door with her finger on the light switch.

"Miss Millie..."

She turned around and looked at me, dark eyes that held no darkness and probably never would.

"Thank you, Miss Millie," I said softly, "Thanks for letting me in."

She had the gentlest kind of smile and she was generous with it. She offered it to me once more.

"Well, you're as welcome here as you feel," she said, "But you ain't gotta call me Miss Millie."

"I think I do, ma'am."

She shut out the light and went softly down the hall and I was asleep before her shadow left the wall. If I dreamed, I didn't remember and I didn't stir from my sleep in the night. When I opened my eyes again, the daylight was sifting through the curtains and the house smelled of coffee, bacon and bread.

I knew that Sneaks was shaving his scruff because I could hear him humming faintly down the hall.

I went out on the porch and had a smoke and two teenage girls passing by on the walk smiled and waved, then giggled together once they passed the gate.

The screen-door creaked open behind me and Sneaks came out with two mugs of coffee and lit the stub of last night's cigar. We smoked and sipped our coffee and the sound of clinking dishes and silverware came from the kitchen.

"C'mon, now," Sneaks said, "Breakfast.

EIGHT
AS WELCOME AS YOU FEEL

I sat with them in their tiny kitchen for the second time and Millie spoiled me forever with the best breakfast I'd ever eaten. The biscuits were tall and flakey; homemade and smothered with gravy whisked right in the pan she'd used to fry the thick slabs of crispy bacon. Instead of potatoes there were grits, buttered and creamy and perfect with salt and pepper and the eggs were fried until the edges were crisp but the yolks were still runny and sweet. Sneaks doused his biscuits and gravy with orange hot sauce and Miss Millie topped off his coffee, then mine, but she drank a cup of black tea.

Millie cleared the dishes from the table and Sneaks went back to the bedroom to get dressed and I sat at the table, sopping up my second plate of biscuits and crunching on the last wide strip of bacon.

"Your clothes are cleaned an' dried an' I packed 'em up nice an' neat in your travelin' bag," Millie said from the sink. "Lord, but you *are* a sloppy packer. Everything all balled up and wrinkled like it was."

I smiled. I couldn't help but smile when she talked.

"I set out a nice suit of clothes for you to put on," she told me, "They's Sneaks' old things an' they'll set a might baggy on you, but you'll look fine enough for church."

Church?

Miss Millie turned around, a patterned dishtowel in her hands and frowned at me gently.

"Well, now...I raised up two boys o' my own and I know *that* face," she said, "Yes, sir, I know the look of a boy that's aimin' to get outta goin' to church on the Lord's own Sunday."

She came and sat at the table.

"I'm gonna ask you the same thing I asked my own sons when they used to get to groanin' 'bout goin' to church instead of goin' fishin' or playin' ball."

She had a sip from her teacup and said, "You got someplace *better* to go?"

I thought of the highway and Huck Finn's river so near and I looked into her honest eyes and couldn't lie.

"No, ma'am, I guess I don't. It's not that. I just...well..."

"Now, there ain't no need for sputterin' an' stutterin'," she said softly, "I told you last night...you're just as welcome here as you *feel*."

I lowered my eyes and told her the truth, though I was sure it would disappoint her.

"I just don't think I believe in God anymore."

She laughed and pushed her chair back from the table and went back to her dishes.

"Well, that's alright, child," she told me, "That don't matter none at all, as long as *He* still believes in *you*. And He surely does."

"But how do you know that, Miss Millie? That God believes in me?"

She looked at me from the sink without a shadow of doubt on her face.

"I know it 'cause if The Lord didn't believe in you, son, you wouldn't a come all this way down all them roads to be standin' here alive in front o' me. You'd be stone dead in some ditch or back alley."

She planted her hands firmly on her hips and I knew that she had won the day and I would be going to church with her and Sneaks.

"Later in the day, Stanley will give you a ride on down the road," she said, 'But this mornin' you're goin' to church."

"Okay, Miss Millie. I'll come, but I don't have nice shoes to wear...just my old boots."

"Well, you'll fit right in then, won't you?"

She laughed and nodded her head toward the kitchen doorway, where Sneaks stood leaning against the wall, tall and straight in a neat brown suit and tie, a handkerchief poking politely out of his breast pocket, a bible tucked under one arm and, of course, those Converse high-top sneakers on his feet.

I went to the back room and found the clothes Millie had left out for me and I put them on: a grey wool suit, a bit long for my arms and legs, a starched white shirt and a thin black tie that I must have fumbled with for too long, because Sneaks and Millie appeared in the doorway to hurry me up.

I told them I was sorry for holding them up, that I didn't know how to knot a necktie and Miss Millie said, "Not to worry. I'll go an' find you a clip-on."

"Nonsense," Sneaks said, "Young man ought to know how to knot a tie."

He stepped across the room, stood close and looked me in my face and taught me how to loop and knot the tie. His bony fingers were paternal and nimble at my bruised neck and I thought of The Troll-Man's fat hand, so deadly around my throat, and in the car on the ride to church, I wondered if maybe Miss Millie was right about God still believing in me.

The church was in better repair than any of the houses we passed on the way, a big, sturdy whitewashed building with a tall steeple and an old-fashion bell and wide doors that were thrown open to welcome in the congregation. Sneaks parked the car beneath a row of shady trees and we walked across the big lawn in front of the church, where men in pressed suits and women in Sunday dresses and pretty hats gathered, talking and laughing. Little kids ran around the churchyard in their best clothes, their mothers hollering after them that they better not get dirty.

As we walked up the stones to the front steps of the church, there were whispers and smiles and open, curious stares. I saw Etta Simms gossiping with a group of elderly ladies and she waved at us as we passed and I heard them talking about me.

"I hear that's his *son* from up in New York City" Etta said and one of the other ladies said, "He do *kinda* look like him...I mean for bein' such a white boy an' all."

Sneaks got a kick out of that and he chuckled and poked his elbow against my ribs.

"That ol' busybody," he said softly, "She don't even believe it *herself*, but she'll go on an' tell it to half the women in the county before the sun goes down."

I laughed and Millie said, "Oh, ain't you two just *terrible*."

At the wide double-doors, we were met with handshakes and smiles, and Sneaks greeted the two men standing on either side of the doorway.

"Hello, Deacon Washington...mornin' to you, Brother Fred."

He introduced me to the men and they welcomed me. One of them clasped my hand in both of his and pumped it up and down and the other patted me on the shoulder and said, "Come right in, now…come *right* on *in*."

We stepped through the doors into a long, straight room with a narrow aisle between rows of polished wooden pews and I thought of country churches I'd seen in old movies. There were hymnals and Bibles on some of the cushions and the people who were already seated when we came in all turned and looked at us and smiled. Some waved at Sneaks and Miss Millie and they waved back and led me down the aisle to the very front row where we sat together at the foot of a small stage with a pulpit and big vases of flowers.

The choir was gathering on the stage, all of them in rustling purple robes, and the pews quickly filled as the congregation came in from the warm morning sun and settled down under the cool, lazy draft of big, whirring ceiling fans.

Deacon Washington and Brother Fred pulled the big doors closed and walked together down the long aisle to the stage, where they sat with a few other men in fancy wooden chairs on either side of the lectern.

On one side of the stage a woman put her fingers to the keys of an upright piano, pounding them hard like Jerry Lee Lewis, and on the other side, another woman sat at an organ and put her own fingers to work as a tall, skinny man in his late thirties, handsome in a black suit and skinny tie, smart in wire-rimmed glasses, got up from one of the fancy chairs and stood at the lectern.

He began to clap his hands and the choir started clapping in time with him and then the whole congregation was clapping and rising to its feet as the piano and organ roared in jubilation. The choir started singing and most of the congregation sang along, too, and it was gospel music, but it was the sound of Memphis and Motown, as if Jesus had been born in Detroit, instead of Bethlehem.

I didn't know the songs, but I was swept to my feet between Sneaks and Millie and I clapped in time with everybody else and sang along with the choruses and catchy refrains, Sneaks' whiskey tenor in my right ear and Millie's honey soprano like an angel in my left. We sang about building on that shore, building for our Jesus, building evermore and about a home in Glory Land that outshines the sun. Nearly everybody danced, some shuffling in place where they stood and others sliding and bouncing in the aisle and up on the stage.

Tarnished metal plates with fancy engraving around the edges were passed up and down the rows and everyone dug in their billfolds, pockets or purses and *everyone* gave *something*, folded bills or jangling coins, and sang with faithful hope that their names would be remembered when that roll is called up yonder in the Lord's sweet by and by.

As the plate was passed hand to hand down our row, I reached into my pocket and pulled out my thin fold of money. I had twenty-seven dollars and I thought I could spare the two singles, but when the plate came from Millie to me, I peeled off a five-dollar bill and sent it on its way, wondering how much of God's work a measly offering like mine would afford.

The music settled down to a sweet pastoral melody, the choir and congregation settled into their seats and the preacher leaned forward, settled his hands on the corners of the pulpit and smiled into a microphone that he really didn't need.

"Good mornin', good mornin' and welcome," he said, his voice rich and thick and smoky, "It's good to see you all this mornin' gathered in the house of God!"

He looked straight down at me and said, "It's good to see a new face, too," and I felt my skin blush warm, but Millie patted my knee with her soft hand and Sneaks mumbled, "That's right, Preacher."

I didn't feel embarrassed, just welcomed and loved and shy. The preacher smiled at Sneaks and said, "Won't you lead us all this mornin' in a word of prayer?"

Sneaks stood and clasped his hands in front of him and we all followed him to our feet, bowed our heads and closed our eyes. Sneaks cleared his throat and began to pray, asking God in his bourbon drawl for mercy, forgiveness and blessings and I wasn't surprised at all that he could speak about the things of heaven as naturally as he did about the art of hoo-ha kissing. He finished with "and keep us from harm in our travels…in Jesus' name…amen" and the congregation joined in on the last word and we all sat down once more.

The preacher flipped through the pages of a big black bible and said, "If you turn with me now to the book of Matthew, chapter 20…we'll see what the Lord has to share with us today."

There were quiet murmurs and rustling pages as the congregation flipped through their Bibles. I didn't have a book of my own, but Millie opened hers on her knee and I leaned over and followed her finger along the text as the preacher spoke.

"Now, here we are with Jesus and his disciples and, in the previous chapter, they come out of Galilee and into the land of Judaea…"

He wandered away from the pulpit, leaving the microphone behind and he walked back and forth on the stage and talked about how multitudes had followed Christ into Judaea and been healed by His hands. His voice carried through the church and he waved his hands and stomped his feet as he told us first how the Pharisees came with temptation and tricks, then how the little children came and were scolded by the disciples, but Jesus took them to Him and blessed them all.

"And you know what Jesus says at the end of that scripture, friends?"

His voice had reached a dramatic pitch and he gasped on the end of his question and rocked back and forth on his feet, three-parts John the Baptist and one-part James Brown.

I remembered the fevered sermon that Reverend Johnson Beal had given on the radio and wondered if he and this country preacher even believed in the same God. Beal had sounded hysterical, accusing and self-righteous, like a man who loves the sound of his own voice and talks mostly just to hear it, but the young preacher on the stage was different. His tone held no accusations, his eyes were empty of pride and he shouted, but never screamed.

"He says 'many that are first shall be last, and the *last* shall be *first*!'"

There were quiet encouragements (*come on now, preacher*) and muffled agreements (*amen, amen, that's right*) from the congregation. The preacher stood at the very edge of the stage and looked from face to face.

"That's what *Jesus* said, folks. He said the first will be last and the last *will* be first...and here in the twentieth chapter of the book of Matthew, He tells us a story about workers in a vineyard, but we know The Lord speaks in parables and so we know He's not really talking about a vineyard at all, but the servants of God and the Kingdom of Heaven."

He roamed the stage as he preached and even came down the short steps to stand among the congregation, telling a story about a man who hired workers to tend his vineyard. Some of the workers were hired in the early morning and they toiled all day, but others were hired in the afternoon and evening and came late to the fields, to work just part of the day. When the work was done and the man paid the laborers, those who'd come in the morning were angry that they had been paid the same wage as the workers who'd joined them later.

"And they murmured against the good man of the house," the preacher said, "And he told them all they'd been paid just exactly what had been promised and sent them on their way, paying the very last man exactly the same as he paid the first."

He stepped softly back to the pulpit and closed the Bible.

"You see, friends...it doesn't matter *when* you come to Jesus. You might be someone who grew up in the Church and you've been *saved* since you were a small child, or you may be a body who come to God in your old age, but I promise you, brothers and sisters, that the reward in Heaven is the same for each and every one of us."

His eyes wandered over the congregation and settled on mine for a moment, or at least I imagined they did.

"You might be a sinner all your days and hold out 'til the end and only come to God on your deathbed of fear, but I'm tellin' you *here* and *now*, you'll be welcomed in Heaven, just the same."

The piano and organ roared back to life and the choir sang about an old rugged cross as the congregation stood, some filing back out into the warmth of the day, others milling about and talking in the emptying church.

Sneaks crossed the room and spoke with the preacher at the end of the stage and I stood waiting with Miss Millie. She introduced me to a smiling round woman in a wide red hat and a pretty young girl in a flower-print dress, who blushed and said "How do you do?"

The church had nearly emptied when Sneaks came back across the room and we walked up the aisle and out the front door where the preacher was standing at the top of the steps, shaking hands and patting backs as his congregation passed on their way back home.

When our turn came, he shook my hand, but he met Sneaks with a warm embrace.

"Real fine preachin'," Sneaks said through his shining smile, "*Real* fine preachin' today."

"Thank you, Daddy," the preacher said softly. He hugged Millie and kissed her cheek and said, "Momma, ain't you *always* just the prettiest girl in church."

Others were crowding behind us and we moved along down the steps and followed the stones across the lawn toward the big, full trees and the car.

I looked at Millie and smiled.

"He's your *son*," I said, "The preacher's your son."

Miss Millie laughed and waved her hand, careful not to boast.

"Oh, you'd be surprised what a boy can turn out to be, if you pester him into church when he'd rather be out messin' around."

"What about your *other* son, Miss Millie? Does he still go to church?"

Sneaks leaned against the car and sighed softly, glanced across the churchyard at a low stone wall.

"He surely does; every single day," she said, "Stanley Junior is buried just over yonder in the cemetery behind the church-house."

NINE
BLESSED

Miss Millie handed me a long mother's hug and a brown paper sack and sent me to the car, where Sneaks sat waiting to take me down the road.

"That's two big ham san'wiches for you," she said, "And a *homemade* pickle"

She stood on the back porch with one hand on her hip and the other waving in the air as Sneaks backed the big Lincoln out of the dusty yard and onto the hard dirt road. I got out of the car and closed the chain-link gate and Millie hollered across the dooryard.

"You be careful now an' find your place, child! The Good Lord ain't give up on you *yet*."

I smiled at her smile, but my eyes were suddenly wet and warning of tears. I put on my cheap sunglasses and blew her a kiss from the palm of my hand.

"Thanks, Miss Millie," I called out, "Thanks a lot for *everything*."

"You're always welcome back here," she said, "If you come on down through this way again."

"Just as welcome as I *feel*," I said

"That's right," Millie agreed, "But if you show up on Sunday, your skinny white butt is goin' to *church*."

I told her goodbye, got in the car and Sneaks drove us past the rows of houses and the corner market and out onto the highway, the radio turned up and the windows rolled down. He lit a cigar and said, "Well, now you're off again, bound for the mighty Mis'sip."

"Gotta keep walkin' off my blues, right?"

I smiled at him, but my smile didn't take and I frowned and said, "I'm sorry I asked about your other son, Sneaks. I didn't know."

He smiled and shook his head and puffed his cigar.

"Well, 'course you didn't know and you meant no harm in askin' after him."

He drove for a few minutes in silence, his eyes staring straight out over the big steering wheel, chewing on the end of his cigar.

"Junior was a wild kind o' boy, a bit of a travelin' man like yourself. Oh, mind you, he never went away as far as California or nothin' but he used to wander up to Memphis and down to the Gulf Coast. He never had much more than a change o' clothes and his ol' guitar. Never seemed to want for much else, neither."

I looked at Sneaks.

"He was a bluesman, wasn't he?" I said, "A real one."

"Yes, sir…that's just what he was; a born bluesman," Sneaks said, "An' he died like one, too. He got himself shot in the backroom of some juke-joint, killed over a woman or money or dope. Maybe all three. Don't know which it was and I s'pose it don't much matter."

I said what people always say, the smallest words of all.

"I'm sorry, Sneaks. I'm sorry Stanley Junior got killed."

"That boy was a hell of a singer, a *hell* of a singer. Used to stay out all night Saturday swampin' and bluesin' and *still* show up on time to sing like an angel in church come Sunday mornin'."

"I bet Miss Millie liked that," I said.

"Oh, you know she did! That woman always saw both sides of a person. Always loved both sides, too. She used to say that gospel music was just the blues once you give 'em over to The Lord."

I smiled.

"You married a good woman, Sneaks."

"Ain't none better," he said softly, "Prettiest ol' gal in four counties, too!"

He took a long puff from his cigar and looked at me with certainty and sadness in his eyes.

"A momma always loves her son," he said, "No matter what kind of trouble a boy gets up to."

We had been talking about Miss Millie and Junior, but I knew that he was trying to tell me something about myself and my own mother.

"You ought to *remember* that, bluesman," he said softly, "Remember it an' don't you ever forget it."

We drove into the afternoon, through the shadows of the trees and the sunlight that snuck between them and soon I could see the Mississippi, wide and brown and lazing through the valley. Sneaks steered the car to a stop on the dusty shoulder of the road.

"Well, young man...it's been a fine day knowin' you."

He reached into his shirt pocket, pulled out an envelope and handed it to me.

"That's a little somethin' to ease you down the road."

The envelope was thick with money. I thumbed the edges of the bills and slid the envelope back across the seat.

"I can't take this much money from you, Sneaks," I said, "That's over three hundred bucks."

Sneaks laughed.

"Boy, that ain't *my* money! That come from the church," he said, "A little bit from the offerin' plates. My boy Calvin an' the Deacons...they all agreed on givin' you a bit o' help."

I shook my head and thought of what I'd said to Miss Millie earlier that morning (*I just don't think I believe in God anymore*) and her laughing, loving reply.

"I still can't take it, Sneaks," I said, "It's too much to take, *especially* from the church."

Sneaks sighed and pushed his sunglasses up on his forehead. "How much money you got in your pockets, son?" he asked me. "Tell me true, now."

"Twenty-two bucks," I mumbled.

Sneaks whistled through his teeth.

"Twenty-two dollars! That's all you got, but you dropped a five-dollar bill in the collection plate this mornin'. I seen that, and so did The Lord."

"That was just..."

"Hush up and listen to me, boy," Sneaks said softly, "That was an *offerin'* is what it was. You give an' offerin' to God an' everything you give to God, well, He's gonna bless you right back for it."

He pushed the envelope back into my hand.

"Sometimes you might have to wait for that blessin' and get to doubtin' you're ever gonna get it at all," he told me, "Other times, God just slaps it right back to you in a flash. Either way you *get* your blessin', you ought not deny it when it comes."

I folded it into my pocket.

"You shoulda been a preacher, Sneaks."

He shook his head and laughed and puffed his cigar.

"Oh, I s'pose if I'd took to preachin', they'd have made me give up my old sneakers by now."

"That wouldn't do," I said, and Sneaks agreed.

"No, sir...wouldn't do at *all*."

I got out of the Lincoln and grabbed my pack from the back seat and Sneaks passed my sack lunch out the window.

"Don't go forgettin' Millie's sammiches or she's like to hunt you down all the way through Mississippi."

He smiled that unbelievably white smile and stuck his skinny arm out the window to shake my hand.

"You be safe now, an' you keep that cash money close."

He nodded toward the river and the bridge just ahead and the buildings on the other side, barely visible through the trees.

"That's Greenville, Mis'sippi yonder 'cross the river," he said, "It's a big town an' you stick out like a sore thumb 'round here, so you watch yourself goin' around down there."

"I will, Sneaks."

He sat there behind the big steering wheel, his head cocked out the window and he sighed.

"I know it don't seem so to a fella your age, but life ain't ever so long as we expect it to be," he told me quietly, "You can run down that ol' road 'til you're as dried up an' dusty as me an' come to find out, all along it was a snake what swallowed you whole."

I didn't know what to say to that so I grinned, but it faltered.

"An', boy...just one more thing, now. You don't go drinkin' corn liquor with strangers."

This time my smile came of its own free will and I said, “No, sir. Never again. I swear it.”

“Well, then,” he sighed, “What’s left to say?”

“Just goodbye,” I told him. “Thanks for everything, Sneaks.”

He smiled and dropped the car into gear and said, “Well, you’re just about as welcome as you can be, bluesman.”

He swung the big Lincoln around and pointed it west and I stood on the side of the road and watched it disappear around a bend, into those shimmering, secretive trees. I slung my pack and turned toward the river and I noticed the way the trees leaned away from the road at the mouth of the bridge, and I thought of a snake, with steel girder fangs and a black asphalt tongue, yawning to swallow me whole.

TEN
FULL-SERVICE

There was a Texaco station across the highway, a small garage with just four pumps and no market, but there was a soda machine out front and they sold cigarettes. There was a girl sitting on a bench in front of the station, a small patterned overnight bag between her feet, and she watched me as I crossed the road. A man in greasy coveralls came out of the garage, wiping his hands on a red rag, and met me at the pumps.

"Afternoon," he said.

He looked to be in his late fifties, tall and broad, with wavy grey hair and still brown eyes. He glanced at my duffel bag and my boots.

"What can I do you for, friend?"

He said it like a man who calls everybody his friend, especially if they might have some money to spend at his service station, but I could tell he didn't care much for me showing up without a car, hauling a pack on my shoulder.

"Just some cigarettes," I told him.

I dropped my duffel to the ground and reached in my pocket.

"And some change for the soda machine."

He sighed softly and I imagined he was thinking the transaction was hardly worth wiping the grease off his hands.

"Sure thing," he said, "Come on inside."

"I can get 'em somewhere else, if it's a hassle?"

He didn't like my tone any more than I liked his, but he stuffed the rag in his pocket and nodded at the garage.

"Ain't no hassle," he said, "I just get busy is all, runnin' a full-service station.

I followed him across the lot to the garage, where the soda machine and the bus stop bench crowded the curb. The girl stood up from the bench and grinned.

"You ridin' the bus, too?" she said, "I'm goin' up to Starkville."

I shook my head.

"No, I'm not ridin' the bus. I don't like 'em much."

She smiled. She was sixteen or seventeen years old, cute and curvy in a Stevie Nicks tee-shirt.

"Oh," she said, pointing at my duffle bag, "I thought you were ridin' the bus, what with your luggage and all."

"I'm just hitchin' through."

I followed the man into the station and he stepped behind a low counter.

"You say you're hitchin' rides?" he said, "Lots o' shady folks out on the road these days, don'tcha think?"

I thought of The Troll-Man and other threatening men I'd met along the road, but there had been far more good people than bad ones behind the wheels of all the cars and trucks I'd climbed into or under the bridges and trees where I had slept.

"There are some," I told him, shrugging my shoulders, "Mostly people treat me pretty decent."

He stared at me and I realized that he had probably been talking about me, not he people who picked me up, when he mentioned shady people on the road. I asked him for two packs of Pall Mall and he reached under the counter for the cigarettes and set them beside the register. He rang up the sale and I peeled a ten out of the envelope, handed it across the counter and asked him for two dollars in quarters.

"We got a bus that stops here on its way over the bridge to Greenville," he said, handing me my change, "It's comin' through in just about an hour. They'll sell you a ticket right on the bus."

"I'm not goin' far today," I said, "I'm just gonna walk down by the river. Maybe camp out for the night."

He whistled and held the door open for me on our way outside.

"Well, you sleep with one eye open if you go an' do *that*," he said, "Got shady folks down in the woods there, doin' dope and drinkin' and who knows what. Mostly over on the Greenville side, but we get 'em right down the bank here, too, sometimes."

I didn't think he was warning me about bad folk on the river so much as he was lumping me in among them.

"State cops run 'em out now an' then," he said, "But they just *come* back again."

He yanked the greasy red rag out of his back pocket and honked his nose into it. I mumbled something about keeping to myself and traded four quarters for two cans of Coke from the machine.

The bus stop girl said, "Can I have one of those cigarettes?"

I slid one of the Pall Malls out of the box and she took it and held it between her lips, her hands cupped around the end while I lit it.

"You want a soda?" I said.

She glanced at the vending machine.

"They got Dr. Pepper?"

I fed two more coins into the slot and pressed the button. I handed her the can of soda and she popped the top and took a long swallow, followed by a long drag from the cigarette and a long, leaning look at my face.

"You're wearin' an earring in your ear," she smiled, "You don't see much o' that around here."

I laughed.

"You know...that's what *everybody* keeps tellin' me."

Well, I *like* it," she said, "Say...where you hitchin' to?"

I lit a cigarette, shrugged and glanced at the bridge to Mississippi.

"I dunno. Wherever I end up, mostly."

She squinted at me and her forehead crinkled up. "Well, where you hitchin' *from*?"

"Everywhere," I said, "Just about everywhere."

"You a *runaway* boy?" she asked me, "You run away from home or the work farm or somethin'?"

"I ain't a runaway," I said, "Not anymore."

"What happened to your eye?" she said, "And your neck?"

"A troll-man got me," I told her.

"A troll-man?" she said, "That don't even make any *sense*."

I stuffed the two cans of Coke into my pack, right on top next to the bag of ham sandwiches, and slung the duffel over my shoulder. She hollered after me as I walked back out to the highway.

"Shame you ain't ridin' the *bus*! We could ride in the back and make out."

I grinned, waved at her over my shoulder and followed the highway out onto the bridge and across the wide river, out of Arkansas and into Mississippi. It was a long walk on a narrow strip of concrete and every passing car seemed to rush by near enough to blow me over the low rail and down into the churning, muddy water below.

ELEVEN
MISSISSIPPI SHAKEDOWN

On the Mississippi side of the bridge, I slid down a grassy slope to the wooded banks of the river and followed a thin path beneath the trees. I sat on my pack in a small clearing and ate the lunch Millie had packed for me. The sandwiches were thick and meaty with mayonnaise and mustard and pepper and the homemade pickle was crisp and sour, The Cokes had gone a little warm in my pack, but I drank one down just the same.

The afternoon had grown long and the sun burned far away across the river, but it was cool near the water, in the shadows of the trees. I leaned against a mossy stump with a cigarette between my lips, listening to the working day sounds of Greenville above me and humming boats passing by on the river just below.

I heard a rumbling motor, low on the breeze, and I glanced up the river and saw a big bus, gleaming in the long, late sun, passing over the bridge on its way into Mississippi. I thought of the pretty girl in the rock and roll tee-shirt, on her way up to Starkville and, wistfully, of a cozy bench-seat at the back of the bus and the kiss of a girl who'd be a memory by morning.

I dug through my jacket pockets and found the little stash of pot I had left, rolled a thin joint and smoked until my head felt a little lighter, my eyes a little heavier and my mouth so dry and dusty that I drank the second warm soda in just a couple of big swallows.

I rummaged through my duffel, careful of the clean clothes that Miss Millie had folded and packed so neatly, and pulled out my notebook; a hundred sheets of paper, curling at the corners and stained by coffee, sweat and rain. I kept a black felt tip pen tucked in the spiral binding and I took it to the first blank sheet and scrawled 'BROKEN BOTTLE' across the wide upper margin.

I came upon a stranger
Underneath a bridge one night
Drinking from a broken bottle
His lips were bloody red
And I sat down with him
And said the rain had driven me
From the open highway
Here to where he'd made his bed
He passed me the bottle
It would warm me up, he said

I wrote and the world around me shrunk away until it was small enough to fit within the pages of my notebook. The sounds from the town, the river and the road hushed beneath the whispers of the memories I'd stirred. I remembered the moldy cellar underneath the narrow bridge and I could see the crackling fire, smell The Troll-Man's sour feet. In my head, I heard his goblin giggle and the riddle he'd whispered of milkmen and murder, but I didn't hear the boys tramping through the brush until they were close upon me and one of them spoke, calling me out of the notebook and back to the riverside.

"Whatcha writin' there, boy?"

There were three of them; boys my age or near enough to it, and they stood in close around me where I sat on my pack with my back to the big, hollow stump. Two of them were brothers for sure, tall and strong with the same blonde hair and mean, narrow eyes. The third boy was thinner and five feet tall at most. His hair was brown and his resemblance to the others was so vague that he might have been a cousin or a just a neighbor whose eyes were only mean and narrow by coincidence.

I stood up, folded the notebook closed with my left hand and my right hand went loosely to my hip, adding weight to the knife on my belt. The skinny boy lunged at me and shoved me against the stump. He snatched the notebook from my hand and stepped back nearer to his mean-eyed friends and I wrapped a sweaty grip around my knife, but didn't draw it.

"*Poems!*" he snorted, "He's writin' *poems*!"

I kept my hand on the pommel of my knife, reached forward and grabbed the notebook out of his hands and the biggest of them laughed and said, "He's a *poet* an' he don't even know it."

They all laughed, like a trio of crows, and the little, bony kid grinned at his friends and sneered at me.

"I wrote a poem once. On the bathroom wall down to the Burger Shack."

I let the notebook fall from my fingers and glanced from one face to the next, settling on the skinny one, not because he was the smallest, but because he seemed to be the smartest and meanest of the bunch. He was the one the others followed.

"Why don't you just go on back up the river?" I said, "Mind your own, like I'm minding mine."

He looked at the bigger boys, the brothers who might have been his cousins, and then he squinted back at me.

"Look at that, boys," he said through a slippery grin, "He's got a big ol' earring in his ear! Looks like some kinda fag, sittin' down here writin' his poems."

There was no way out of it except into it and I took a step toward him with my fists raised up and the three of them were on me all at once. The biggest boy wrapped his arms around me and held me from behind, while the other two ploughed their fists into my belly and the skinny one planted a hard one on my mouth.

"Don't worry yourself, *faggot*," he said, "We don't want your stupid poems."

I kicked out at him with my boots, but he stepped back in the dust and the big boy's grip tightened around my chest then slackened just a little as a girl's voice hollered out.

"Bobby-Ray Dearman! You let that boy go and y'all lay off o' him!"

Bobby-Ray didn't let me go, but he lowered his hands to hold me by my forearms and the other two boys turned to look at her. The girl in the Stevie Nicks t-shirt stood with her hands planted on her hips, glaring straight into the skinny boy's narrow eyes.

"You *heard* me, Donny Dodge. You an' your cousins just lay right off him now, before I get my daddy."

Bobby-Ray let me go and shoved me against the stump and Donny glared at the girl.

"Just shut your mouth, Roselyn!" he said, "Your daddy's a part-time reserve deputy. Ain't like he's the *sheriff* or anything."

She cocked her head and smiled.

"That don't mean he won't come down here and whoop your skinny ass if I tell him he *ought* to."

Bobby-Ray looked at his brother and shrugged his big shoulders, then he looked at his scrawny cousin.

"C'mon, Donny..." he grumbled, "Her daddy might not come down here an' whoop us, but he'd tell the sheriff *for sure*. I ain't goin' back to any work farm."

Donny sneered at me and wiped the back of his hand across his forehead.

"Best not hang around here too long, boy," he threatened, "Next time I see you...might not be a *girl* around to save you."

"Yeah," I told him. "Maybe it'll just be me and *you*."

Bobby-Ray nudged his brother up the path and through the trees and their cousin followed behind them. I slumped down on my pack and looked up at Roselyn.

"You missed your bus."

"Ain't that lucky for you," she smiled, "Those boys meant to beat you up an' rob your money."

I pushed my hair up off of my forehead, shook two cigarettes loose from the pack and Roselyn sat beside me and leaned against the stump. I lit both of the smokes and passed one to her, took a deep pull on my own and tried to blow smoke rings.

"Why would they think I have money...or even know I was down here?"

"That big mouth Ernest Tucker at the fillin' station," she said, "Folks 'round here ain't got *enough* to talk about. Those boys come around for a Coke and Ernest about burst tellin' us all what a fool you were, goin' down along the river with a big wad o' money in your pocket."

I sighed and shook my head and she blew cigarette smoke in my face.

"Well, I *know* those boys. The Dearman brothers are stupid, but they're big an' they do 'bout whatever Donny tells 'em they ought to. I knew what he was schemin' to do an' I followed 'em down here when they come to find you."

"What about the bus to Starkville?"

She told me she could catch another bus in the morning.

"That bus only stops at the Texaco so folks don't have to walk across the bridge to catch it at the depot. It only comes through once a day but they got three or four buses out of Greenville. My momma won't care if I come today or tomorrow or not at all."

I smashed my cigarette out in the dirt.

"What you gonna do tonight then? Go on home?"

Her smile was shy, but her eyes were sly.

"Well, I *could* go home," she said, "But my daddy'd be mad that I didn't get on the bus and I'd have to tell him *why* and then he'd prob'ly bring the sheriff down here an' have a look at you."

I shook my head. "I don't need the cops comin' down here."

'Well, we could go into Greenville an' stay the night together," she said softly, "There's a motel right on the highway that don't cost but twenty dollars a night an' right next door, there's a barbecue shack."

She slipped one hand into mine and leaned close and her breath was warm and sweet, her hair smelled of flowers.

"I *did* save your skin, you know...and missed my bus doin' it."

"How old are you?" I said, "How old are you really? Last thing I need is your old man comin' down and draggin' me to jail."

"Don't worry 'bout my daddy," she said, "Remember, he's just a part-time reserve deputy. Besides, I don't tell my daddy *everything*.

The woman in the motel office gave me a hard time about not having any I.D. to prove I was of legal age to sign for the room, but she finally gave in and slid a key across the counter when I told her I'd pay in cash and give her a ten-dollar deposit she could keep. I met Roselyn outside where she sat waiting on the concrete stairs and we walked across the lot to the barbecue joint and came back with big cups of iced tea and a white paper sack of ribs and coleslaw and beans.

In the room we sat barefoot on the bed and ate with the lights out and the television on, licking tangy sauce from our fingers and sipping tea, laughing at a rerun of *Laverne & Shirley*, talking and teasing and touching each other.

We passed a joint between us in the dark and, after, her kisses were smoky and soft. Her hands peeled the shirt off my back and I slid her jeans past the curve of her thighs. Her skin had the soft scent of linen and town that I hadn't known for so long.

We rushed it like only the young ever do and when we were done, we had nothing to say. She slipped from the bed and ran the shower and I fell asleep thinking it was just like the sound of soft rain, and I only woke up for a moment when she got in bed beside me and pulled the blanket up over our legs.

In the morning I woke up early and the side of the bed she'd slept on was empty, the blanket thrown back and tangled, the pillow smashed against the headboard. I rubbed my eyes, sat on the edge of the bed and lit a Pall Mall.

Her patterned overnight bag was gone and my big duffel was crumpled and empty, the clothes Miss Millie had put away so neatly jumbled in a wrinkled pile on the floor. The pockets of my jeans had all been turned out and she'd gone through my jacket and taken my bag of pot and my pipe, too.

She left the envelope that Sneaks had given me torn on the bedside table, with a note written across the flap (*At least I didn't take it all*) and just a single twenty-dollar bill left inside.

She'd made a fool out of me and I should have seen it coming. She'd been as sly as The Troll-Man, but nowhere near as ugly, and she'd stopped the Dodge boy and his cousins when they had only half-way beaten me just so she could rob me herself.

I stalked around the small room, mad about the three hundred dollars and about the mess she'd made of Miss Millie's folding. For a moment I swore I'd hitch up to Starkville and find her, but she was as gone as the money, and I knew it.

TWELVE
MYSTERIOUS WAYS

I had the room for another four hours so, I left the mess alone, put on the clothes I'd worn the day before and shoved the room key and the twenty-dollar bill deep in my pocket. I needed coffee and if the Barbecue Shack wasn't open this early, there was a little place just up the block with big bright windows and neon signs and a giant, spinning donut on the roof.

There was a housekeeping cart in front of the room next to mine and a grey-haired woman stepped out of the open door, a pillow case in one hand and the pillow it belonged to in the other.

"You checkin' out early, honey?" she said, "Should I go on an' change out your room?"

She wore a name-tag pinned to her smock. Her name was Ardith.

"I'm just goin' for coffee," I said. "I'll be comin' back to shower and for my things."

She smiled.

"Oh, I ain't rushin' you, hon. You're paid up 'til ten o'clock. Norm's up on the corner has real good coffee. And the donuts are real fine, too."

I gave her back the smile and said, "I'll tell Norm you sent me. Could I bring you back a cup?"

"Oh, I don't drink but one cup a day and I've had that," she said, "But I'd trouble you for one of those cigarettes. "

I gave her one and lit another for myself and we leaned against the black metal railing and smoked.

"Did you see a girl leave out of here this morning?" I asked her, "Out of my room?"

She talked with the cigarette dangling from the corner of her mouth.

"Well, I seen a girl come down the stairs *real* early...maybe 4 o'clock," she said, "I was changin' rooms on the ground floor. I couldn't say she come from your room, but she *did* come down the stairs."

"Pretty girl with a little suitcase?"

Ardith nodded and said, "That your girl? She run out on you?"

"I just met her," I sighed. "She stole my money."

She took a deep drag on the cigarette and shook her head.

"Lord, Lord...you gonna call the police?"

"I don't think so, no."

I told her about the money that the church had given me and the boys who meant to rob me at the river and how Roselyn had seemed to save me, but had only been saving me for herself.

"Even if her dad wasn't a deputy sheriff," I said, "She's still a local girl from town and I'm just a stranger hitch-hiking through."

"I guess that's the hard truth of it then," Ardith said, "But that money come from *God* an' maybe this is exactly what *He* intended for it?"

I laughed.

"God gave me some money so He could take it away?"

"Maybe so, maybe not," Ardith laughed, "I've known The Lord to do all kinds o' crazy things to get a fool's attention."

She stubbed her cigarette out on the railing and looked up at the sky.

"There isn't a one of us down *here* who knows what He's workin' on up *there*," she said, "There's no guessin' how God might use that money..."

She pointed at me and smiled.

"...or how he might use *you*!"

I shrugged, but I didn't bother arguing my lack of faith or telling her that I couldn't think of any use God might have for me, unless he was looking to kill a dog.

"So whatcha gonna do then?" Ardith said, "I mean, after your coffee and your shower?"

I hadn't thought about what I'd do or where I'd go, now that I'd disappointed my mother at Graceland and myself at the Mississippi river. I thought of my mother, a ghost in a dusty dream, scolding me for running away and telling me I had better get home and I answered the housekeeper's question on impulse, before I even realized what I was saying.

"New Jersey. I guess I'm goin' home"

I hadn't been home, or thought of it that way, since 1982. I'd run as far away west as the land would allow and I had been cautious whenever I went east again, in case I accidentally made it back to where I started from.

"How long's it been?" Ardith said, "Since you been home?"

I sighed and told her it had been a long, long time.

"I'm a stranger there now," I said.

Ardith smiled and shook her head and said, "Ain't it *funny* sometimes the way God gives a little nudge?"

I asked her if there was a truck stop in town, somewhere I could catch a long ride and she told me there was one nearby.

"There's a pretty big one over at the junction," she said, "If you can get a ride east on 82, it ain't far; maybe half-way to Indianola, just out on Highway 61."

I gaped at her.

"You didn't just *actually* say the words "out on Highway 61.'"

She looked puzzled and her smile lost its confidence. "Well, sure, that's where the truck stop is. Highway 61."

"Highway 61? *The* Highway 61?"

"Honey, I don't know what you're makin' such a fuss about," Ardith said, "It's the only Highway 61 I know of hereabouts."

"Oh, c'mon..." I said, "You know the song. 'God said to Abraham, kill me a son...'"

She waved her hand in front of her face, as if she were shooing off an imaginary fly.

"That's from the Bible, honey. Book o' Genesis."

"No, ma'am," I argued, "*That's* Bob Dylan."

THIRTEEN
THE BLUES HIGHWAY

When I crossed the bridge from Arkansas the day before, I had meant to follow the Mississippi all the way to the Gulf of Mexico, and let the breezes out of New Orleans decide where I would go from there. In my days on the road, though, I almost never ended up where I set out to go, at least not when I expected or by the route I meant to take.

I had cut south out of Ohio nearly ten days before, bound for Memphis to bury a ghost before heading back west, just to end up looking east down a road that would lead back to my hometown.

You better get home, Richie.

Destination and direction can change as suddenly as the weather and a map is best left unfolded, if a boy wants to follow his soul.

I caught an easy ride out of Greenville, eastbound on 82, and left the Mississippi behind me, abandoning my childhood brother Huck Finn for a truck stop on the edge of a blue highway and a homesick wind whispering north, and by the early afternoon, I climbed out of the bed of a Ford pickup truck and stood on the side of the road beneath a black and white highway sign.

There was another sign further up the ramp, warning pedestrians off the highway and I knew a sign like that meant that I was likely to catch a ticket if a cop found me walking along the shoulder.

Walking on a highway can be a tricky thing, not just avoiding being hit by a truck, but avoiding trouble with the law. Some highways you can walk along and not break any laws and others, like the freeways and the Interstates, you couldn't walk on at all. There were even roads where it was illegal to walk on one stretch of it and just fine to walk another stretch. Sometimes it just came down to the cop. Some would drive right past and leave you to yourself and others would pull up slow and stop you, to write you a ticket or just as an excuse to run your name. I had caught a few tickets along my way and even ended up in jail once for walking on an

Arizona highway. I decided not to push my luck in Mississippi and I dropped my pack at the foot of the sign.

The back-side of the sign was a hitch-hiker's bulletin board, covered with names, dates and epitaphs from dozens of different hands. You can tell an on-ramp or junction where a lot of tramps passed by checking the backs of signs to see how many had written on it and what they had to say.

The grey metal diamond was crowded, but I dug my marker out of my bag and left a message of my own written on the wooden signpost.

Rick Holeman Apprentice Hoo-Ha Kisser

I didn't know enough about blues music to know how much of its history was paved into the blacktop lanes of Highway 61. I grew up on my mom's fifties music and top-40 a.m. radio and grew into more serious rock & roll songwriters in my teens. I was still learning from them about the blues and old folk songs that told the secret history of America. What I knew about Robert Johnson and his deal with the devil, I'd heard second-hand from Eric Clapton, and all I knew of Highway 61 was Dylan's fabled road of red, white and blue shoe-strings where God could kill a child and you could engage in all sorts of things that you never had before.

As it was, I didn't see the famous American Blues Highway from the ground and I didn't get to sleep beneath its bushes or hear its swampy songs in the roadhouses along the way. I went north riding high on the passenger side of a loaded Freightliner with a friendly east Texas cowboy who picked me up on his way out of the truck stop and promised me a good, long ride.

"Well, I can't get you all the way to *Jersey*," he said with a grin, "But I can get you all the way on up into Kentucky by tonight."

I climbed into the cab and we traded names with a handshake and rolled and rumbled north with Merle Haggard on the tape-deck and the windows down to catch the breeze. We talked a little on the way, but Harold Potts wasn't the kind of driver who asked a lot of questions and the quiet miles didn't seem at all uncomfortably long. I sat with my elbow out the window and my face turned to the wind and Highway 61 blurred before and behind us, a long thin strip of blacktop that straddled the present and past, paving over mystery and history alike for the comfort of the people in the cars just rushing through.

There were plaques along the roadside and we passed peeling taverns and leaning old juke-joints, noisy places where the blues had been born, and tacky neon tourist traps where they were packaged cheap and sold. At the junction with route 49, there was a tower of guitars with a sign that marked the legendary crossroads where Robert Johnson had once stood in the dust and traded his soul for a record contract from Hell.

"Most folks would lay money down and say that ain't the actual spot," Harold said with a chuckle, "But that don't stop all them tourists from crowdin' up an' gettin' their picture took in front of them godawful guitars."

"I wonder what Robert Johnson would think of that," I said.

Harold Potts snorted and chuckled.

"Robert Johnson? Shit-fire, I wonder what *the devil* makes of it all."

We drove on north and crossed into Tennessee and traded the highway for Interstate 40 in Memphis. I'd been in Memphis just five days before, but it seemed long ago, before The Troll-Man and Sneaks and my chance encounter with Stevie Nicks' thieving number-one fan.

I slept a little while, woke up north of Nashville and the number on the highway signs had changed from 40 to 65.

"I'm glad you got some sleep," Harold said, "I'm gonna have to drop you outside Bowling Green, before I pull up to the yard. Comp'ny don't like us takin' on riders."

I climbed down from the Freightliner, pulled my pack down behind me, and gave Harold Potts a wave. He eased the big tractor-trailer back on the road, steered it through a tight left turn and down a block of industrial buildings.

FOURTEEN
DIRTY WORK

I sat on my duffel bag, smoked a cigarette and plotted a loose course to New Jersey by map and memory.

From this end of the line, it looked to be a lean hitch, almost a thousand miles with less than twenty dollars in my pocket and one can of chili and a few strips of jerky in my bag. I'd made longer runs with less and shorter trips with more and I knew that between the first step and the last, everything is temporary, anything can change, and I could cross the country on a dollar and a dime.

Eight days in the south and I'd had all of the hospitality I could live through. My time with Sneaks and Millie had been a warm retreat from a darkened road, but it had left me with a homesick feeling. The sex with Roselyn, though she'd robbed me while I slept, had made me homesick, too; the way that closeness can when you spend all of your time alone.

On the road, I had been alone, but seldom lonesome and I never felt I'd lost my way as long I kept trying to find it, and I wondered if my long journey was coming to an end, not somewhere out in the wild west, but on a highway back to all that I had run from.

It was too early in the evening to find a place to camp and too late in the day to catch a ride from the industrial edge of town. I would have better luck at another ramp and I shouldered my pack and walked north along a frontage road that ran beside the Interstate. I passed empty lots and cinder-block buildings, rows of old houses and neighborhood stores and stopped into a Gulf station to buy a Pepsi and a pack of smokes.

When I came out of the station, a phone-booth caught my eye and I leaned inside the glass and took the receiver from its cradle. There was a click on the line and I pushed 0 then dialed a number from memory and after another click, I heard the operator's voice from some tin-can place far away.

"Collect call from Richard," I told her.

"One moment, please."

Down the line, beneath the buzz of long-distance, a telephone rang in New Jersey and before it rang a second time, I heard another voice on the line. I had been hoping my brother would answer the phone, but my aunt had picked up the call.

"Collect call from Richard," the operator told my aunt, "Will you accept the charges?"

There was another harsh click on the line, but it came from the back of my aunt's throat, not from the crackle of the long-distance wires.

"No," she said, "I goddamned will *not* accept the charges!"

"I'm sorry, sir..." the operator said as I hung up the phone, "Your party's refused the..."

CLICK!

It wouldn't be much of a homecoming, returning to a place where I was still unwanted.

A few more blocks up the road, I met an old man on the sidewalk and he asked me if I could spare a smoke. I gave him one and he popped it between his lips.

"How's about a light?" he said.

He was clean-shaven, but his clothes were dusty and he wore a long coat, too warm for the weather, and a hat so old and battered that it flopped to the side of his head and the brim drooped down over his eyes. He lit the cigarette, slipped me back my lighter and said, "You goin' over to the church for supper?"

I cocked an eyebrow.

"I don't know anything about it," I told him, "But I'm hungry."

"Well, they's servin' supper right around the corner," he said, "You gotta listen to some preachin', but the grub ain't so bad as you'd 'spect it to be."

He clapped me on the shoulder and said, "C'mon an' walk along with me, kid."

I walked along with him, around the corner and down the block, and we joined a group of men, lined up along the red brick wall of a church and he told me his name was Albert.

"They let the women an' kids go in first," he said, "That's why it's just us men in line."

Inside, I took up a tray and a spoon from a stainless-steel cart and a man in a hair-net slapped a slice of bread on the tray and ladled a chunky beige stew over the top of it. I thanked him and nodded at the woman next to him and she smiled and spooned a pile of pale green beans onto the corner of my tray.

I followed Albert past another cart where we each took a pint carton of milk and sat across from him at a long table. The room was crowded and noisy with dozens of different conversations and a rail-thin old man stood at a podium, talking loudly to make his message heard above the chatter.

He didn't have the rousing flair of Sneaks' son Calvin and there wasn't a gospel choir or room enough to dance, but he wasn't full of hateful spit like the radio preacher, either. He spoke with a plain conviction, whether anyone listened or not.

The milk was ice cold and I drank it in one long pull and the stew was hot and thick, but it tasted as beige as it looked. I ate a spoonful that wrinkled my nose and Albert leaned across the table and pulled a small bottle out of his coat pocket.

"Slop some o' this on it, kid. Won't make that shit-on-a-shingle taste any better, but it'll give it a kick in the pants."

I shook the bottle over my tray and stirred the bright red sauce into the stew and flicked a few drops over the green beans, too. The sauce was deadly spicy and I ate with sweat trickling through my hair and down the back of my neck while the preacher spread his news to the toughest crowd in town.

"It's easy when times are hard. It's easy to walk along with the devil when you got troubles and it's easy to believe the things he whispers when you're down and you're out."

His voice crackled out of old speakers, mounted in the corners of the room.

"Ain't nothin' in this world easier to do in troubled times than to make 'em tenfold worse," he preached, "What we *ought* to do when we're in trouble, when our choices are dark, is we ought to do just once what God would have us do."

He paused and drew a deep breath and said, "That'd throw a funky monkey in the devil's dirty work, now, wouldn't it?"

I thought no one had been paying him any attention, but a chuckle spread around the room and I heard a voice I recognized holler out above the rest.

"Oh, I *like* that! I like that one *a lot!*"

I dropped my spoon onto my tray, splashing stew on my clean shirt, and swung my head around to look from face to face.

Three tables back, he sat squeezed into a chair, a bandage taped across his cheek where I'd swung the broken bottle and cut him three nights before. He was staring at the preacher, stew slopped in his whiskers, smiling that rancid yellow grin, but his expression changed suddenly, as if he could feel my eyes upon him. The Troll-Man turned his gaze from the pulpit and met my own.

He wore the same raggedy clothes he'd had on beneath the narrow bridge. There was a hole in his shirt where I'd stuck the bottle's jagged edge into his chest and a dark stain on the cotton where he'd bled.

He stared at me, but his eyes were no longer the dead lanterns of a horny goblin; just the weak, frightened eyes of a fat, filthy man. Whatever black power he had held in the darkness under the bridge drained away from his face in the light of the church. He lowered his eyes, pushed away his tray and got up from the table and ducked out the door in a hurry.

I stood up and grabbed my pack to follow The Troll-Man and Albert called after me.

"Hey!" he shouted, "You gotta clear away your *tray*!"

The small church dining hall was crowded and I squeezed my big duffel bag down the rows between the tables and past a group of men standing in front of the doorway. Outside I looked up the sidewalk and saw The Troll-Man turn the corner, moving fast for the weight he was hauling around, and I followed after him with one hand through the strap of my pack and the other on the handle of my knife.

Murderer or milkman? I guess now we'll know.

He cut into a stand of trees, looking back over his shoulder, and he wiped the back of his hand across his wide forehead. He was slowing down and I was catching up and the trees leaned close and listened in case they were about to witness a secret.

The Troll-Man stumbled down a slope and when he looked back to see if he had been caught yet, his eyes were full of fright. He hollered back at me in a breathless, panting plea.

"You leave me 'lone, you motherhumper! I didn't *mean* it so leave me *alone*!"

I wanted to hurt him, maybe to kill him, not only because he had hurt me or had his filthy fingers under my jeans, but because he had *scared* me, too. I had seen his foul face in *one* dream and expected to dream him again and I chased him through the waking world of the forest because I couldn't chase him out of my sleep.

He smashed his way through thick brush at the bottom of the slope, down where the trees grew thicker and he would soon be out of sight if I didn't hurry after him, but I hesitated. I stood at the top of the hill, imagining I could hear his short, panting breaths and his frightened, jackrabbit heartbeat and my hand went slick and sweaty on my knife.

In my head or on the breeze, I heard the voice of the preacher who had fed us both.

We ought to do just once what God would have us do."

I let The Troll-Man go. I watched him disappear among the whispering leaves and threw a funky monkey into the devil's dirty work.

I had places to go and dirty work of my *own* to tend to.

PART THREE

THE PRODIGAL SON

ONE
CROOKED CROSSES

I camped in the woods east of Bowling Green, down a lonely road marked by old telephone poles that leaned like crooked crosses. In the morning I would chase the highway across Kentucky and out of the south, but that night I built a fire in a wooded hollow, had supper hot from a can and gave up early on Steinbeck. I stowed the book away and listened through the darkness, certain that the hollow I had chosen was a haunted one; even if only because *I* had brought the ghosts.

From my hiding place beneath the trees, I couldn't see any porch lights or glowing windows, but there must have been a house somewhere nearby. Every now and then, a lone dog barked out in the darkness, a gruff and ghostly reminder that the mystery road I had traveled through the south had come full-circle.

Less than fifty miles west, on the other side of the city, there was a blood stain on the road where I had thrown a stone into eternity and caused a good dog's death. Huck was buried there beside a stream. On a farm just beyond Huck's grave, Vernon and Carol Ann lived with a ghost in their house.

I may have taken my detour south back in Ohio, but the journey had really begun on that road where I lost my dog between a car and a stone. Everything before had been a prelude or some kind of warning; at least that's how it seemed.

Luanna had tried to warn me, even if she hadn't known it. She had told me to be mindful about love, then gave me a brief kind of love and went on her way. She had been a sweet reminder to be gentle with goodbyes, but I wasn't and I murdered Huck when he tried to stay.

Before that, there had been another kind of warning, but I hadn't heard it for what it was. The preacher on the radio in Dalton Cummings' truck had been a messenger, too. Johnson Beal had tried to warn me, but his message had been lost in all his screaming rage and wrath. The truth in all his lies had been that God and the devil were near, watching and listening as if neither of them knew that both of them were myths. I might have heard his warning, if he hadn't muffled it with hatred, but even if I'd heard it, I likely wouldn't have heeded it.

I didn't believe in heaven or hell and if I had any religion at all, I was a follower of faithlessness. I carried my shrines in my heart and lived my life close to the earth. I had no church or home, only choices and roads.

The particular road I had chosen was bound to turn bad, the way a road might when it knows you're on your way to see a ghost, and it wasn't the kind of road to travel over alone. I could have used a good companion and I'd had one for a while, but I ran him off forever before I knew what he might mean to me. If Huck had been with me beneath the narrow bridge, he might have saved me from The Troll-Man's filthy hands.

Everything that had happened on that road had been a part of some kind of lesson, and I thought that I had learned it when I met The Troll-Man again, three days after he tried to force me out of my jeans.

I had gone after him in vengeance, but I let him get away and I thought that I had taught myself about mercy, if not forgiveness. I watched him go until he was out of sight and I went along my way with my hands clean. I was sure that in sparing his life, I had spared myself from one more ghost, but that night beneath the darkening trees, The Troll-Man was with me still.

I hadn't been afraid sleeping out since my first restless nights on the road years before, but in the shadowed shelter of the hollow, I was fearful of the darkness. I peered into the black folds of the forest, listening for the sound of something lurking among the trees, wondering if my lesson had yet to be learned.

Maybe it had been a mistake, letting The Troll-Man live. Maybe the lesson hadn't been one about mercy, but a deadlier truth I would learn if he, or another like him, found me again and killed me.

The moon curved across the sky like a searchlight and the electrified crosses on the road cast crooked shadows among the trees. The night was still enough that I could hear another sound above a chorus of crickets; a throbbing, alien buzz. It might have been coming from the high-voltage cables and it may have been the devil humming.

Sleep was a long time coming, but it came.

I dreamed an interstate highway, but it wasn't paved over smooth or marked by lines and lights. Eight lanes of hardened dirt stretched over a ruined landscape of skeleton trees and scorched earth. I walked the southbound shoulder, kicking up dust, and shadowy trucks on the roadway blew by without rumbling or rattling. They shrieked.

The sky was clear and colorless, as washed-out as the fields it overlooked, but on the near horizon, thorny clouds spread on the wind and a distant hum buzzed over the landscape. A strange kind of storm was coming and I would be caught out in it, if I didn't hook a ride.

There was nowhere to shelter along the dirt highway, not a single crumbling barn or fallen-down house where I could hide out from the rain, or dust, blowing in from the east. There was a dead field just off the highway, marked by a barbed-wire fence and a NO TRESPASSING sign, and a scarecrow hung in the distance like a watchman, though there weren't any crows to scare or crops to guard.

Dust blew up around me, the chattering hum on the wind buzzed louder and the blank beige sky went black. The storm was near and I was stranded, lost in a sudden darkness too deep to see through. The moon wasn't out and the stars didn't shine, but twin lights peered through the night and the roar of a V8 engine chased away the shrieking trucks.

The highway emptied for a long, black car that thundered out of the darkness and crouched low along the roadside, growling under its hood, where I knew it hid sharp teeth. The windows were rolled down to the storm and 'Love Me Tender' dripped from the stereo speakers, slow and sweet like honey, but bitter as poison. I knew whose car it was and I stooped to look inside, but instead of the dead king who had stalked me through the south, my mother's ghost sat behind the wheel, wearing the dress she had been buried in.

She was alone in the car and she leaned across the pink bench seat and pushed open the passenger door. A cigarette hung from her mouth and smoke rose in front of her eyes, but she had quit smoking two years before she died.

"You're smoking again."

She shrugged her shoulders and took a deep drag on the cigarette.

"Well, they're sure not gonna kill me," she said, "Now that I'm already dead."

A hard wind rushed between us and the buzzing cloud broke open, spilling a hail of living thorns out on the road.

"Time to go home, Richie," she grinned, "Can't you see it's starting to rain?"

It was raining harder now, not water or dust, but hard, wriggling drops of dread that clung in my hair and crawled over my face. The chattering wind wailed all around us, louder than the sound of my voice, louder than the phantom car's motor, too.

"Where's Elvis?" I shouted.

My mother rolled her eyes and shrugged. Rain was buzzing through the open windows into the car and clots of living dust settled on her shoulders and squirmed through her hair. One fell from her mouth when she shouted back at me.

"I killed him!"

Murderer or milkman?

"Well, not by myself," she admitted, "We *all* killed him. Now, get in the goddamned car."

I backed away from the roadside, glanced over my shoulder at the fallow field and thought I saw the scarecrow moving on his post, beckoning me with a wave. When I turned back to the car, my mother was naked, clothed only with the skittering bugs that had come on the storm.

"What kind of rain is it, Mom?" I hollered, "How come it's alive and you're still dead?"

"It's not a storm," she said, "It's a swarm."

Her eyes went black as rare pearls and she shrieked a single word onto the wind.

"LOCUSTS!"

Her mouth hung open wide, hundreds of bugs rushed into her throat and she screamed until she couldn't make a sound.

I pissed my pants and ran for the fence, leaving my pack in the dust and my blood on the barbs. Blinded by the swarming locusts, I ran through the field with my mouth shut tight, so none of them could crawl inside of me.

I crossed tilled rows of dead soil, where nothing good would ever grow and the chattering wind chased me down with a long, wailing shriek. I thought it was my mother, screaming again, but it must have been the car horn blowing, because her mouth was filled with locusts.

I fled across the darkened field and ran headlong into the scarecrow's post, opening a gash on my forehead and landing my ass in the dirt. I stared up at the straw man and he opened his eyes.

"Where's your milk jugs, boy?"

It wasn't a scarecrow at all, no old, stuffed coat and sackcloth face for frightening birds. It was The Troll-Man up on a cross, alive but crucified. Railroad spikes had been driven through his wrists and ankles and he hung from the beams with his trousers open, his shriveled secret hanging out to the swarm. He wasn't fit for any crown, even one shaped from mean thorns, but his forehead was bloody and bruised, deformed by bony, hooked horns.

"You sure as shit ain't no murderer," he croaked, "So where's your fucking milk jug?"

Among the locust rain, a darker shadow descended and a raven settled on The Troll-Man's shoulder and pecked greedily at the bugs on his face.

I screamed, my mouth filled with locusts and...

I woke up in my bedroll, screaming at the trees and drenched with sweat, the crotch of my jeans soaking wet. I thought I heard the storm still buzzing, but it was only the humming of electric power lines, strung from crooked crosses on the roadside.

In the morning, when I walked out, I avoided looking up at the telephone poles, afraid I'd see The Troll-Man, crucified against the clear, blue sky.

TWO
MOTHERTRUCKER

I had spent most of the twenty dollars Roselyn had left behind when she robbed me, but I splurged for coffee at a truck stop, where I washed up at a men's room sink and changed into clean clothes. The fresh jeans and flannel were wrinkled, the way everything I folded into my duffel ended up, but they still smelled of Miss Millie's detergent and reminded me of her smile and homemade biscuits.

I didn't linger long over my map and coffee, because the waitress was unfriendly and I had heard her complaining to the cook about a cheap stray taking up one of her booths on a busy morning. I had one refill, left a dollar on the table and I didn't feel as cheap as she had made me out to be, leaving a forty-five-cent tip for a fifty-five-cent cup of coffee and lousy service.

Outside, I took up my pack from where I'd stashed it behind a stack of propane tanks, folded away my map and crossed the lot. The sky was clouding over, but it didn't look like rain; the clouds were too thin to be carrying any locusts, or even dust. I followed a sign and a slow line of trucks out to the Cumberland Parkway and before I reached the southbound onramp, I heard the blast of a big rig's airhorn and a Mack truck slowed as it passed and pulled over in the breakdown lane just ahead, taillights flashing to hurry me up. I hitched up my pack and ran, pulled myself up onto the sidestep and yanked open the door to meet the man who had stopped to offer me a ride.

"You're not a man," I said, "You're a lady."

She wore men's work clothes and a rumpled cap, like any other trucker might, but soft curls tumbled out from under her hat and fell on the shoulders of her overalls. She didn't wear any make-up, but she was pretty in a homey way, with soft features and pale green eyes and an open smile.

"You're exactly right about your first point," she said, "And your second one's an optimistic assumption I can live with."

It took me a moment to catch her joke, but I smiled and felt embarrassed.

"Sorry," I said, "I just wasn't expecting a woman truck driver."

She laughed.

"You some kind of male chauvinist already at your age?"

"No, nothin' like that," I told her, "I've just been in hundreds of trucks and never seen a woman driving one of 'em. I don't even think I ever noticed one at a truck stop counter before."

"Oh, there's more women drivin' than you'd think," she said, "Most folks just can't tell us from the men."

We shook hands and her grip was strong, but her palm was soft and she told me her name was Rebecca, but I should call her Becky. She spoke softly and kept the music on the radio at a low volume and the quiet in the truck, with the road whispering and murmuring beneath us, caused me to talk quietly, too.

"What made you wanna be a trucker?" I asked her.

She shook her head and sighed, but it came with a smile and she watched the road ahead with casual caution.

"Never wanted to be one," she said, "This was my husband's truck."

She had been a waitress when she met him, working at a truck stop when he came in off the road and sat in her section. She said he had a smile that stole her heart and a gentle voice that was reassuring and unexpected from a man as big as he had been.

"Howie started comin' in regular," she said, "Sometimes he even changed his route so he could stop in and see me."

Six weeks after they met, she quit her job at the T/A truck stop and went on the road with Howie and two weeks after that, on a run through Las Vegas, they were married in a chapel on The Strip and she became Mrs. Howard Doyle. He took her back to the town he'd been born in and bought her a little house on a shaded lane. He worked the road and bought his own truck and she worked to make the house a place to come home to. One weekend when he was home, he made her pregnant and the weekend after that, he dropped dead on a loading dock in Omaha, Nebraska.

"Heart attack," she said, "He was only thirty-three years old."

He had left her with a mortgage and seven years of fat truck payments and there hadn't been any insurance because they thought that they were both too young to die. She could sell the truck and take a loss, sell the house and rent an apartment and raise her son on a waitress' tips or she could do what Howie had done and work the road. Most of her husband's accounts had stuck by her and she picked up new ones to replace the ones that hadn't.

"I already knew how to drive the truck," she said, "He taught me when I went on the road with him, just for fun, but..."

Her words trailed off and she wiped her eyes with the back of her hand and I felt guilty that she was crying a little from telling me how she had come to be a trucker.

"But it isn't fun anymore," I finished for her.

She shook her head.

"It is sometimes," she said, "But it's hard and tiresome and it's making me old. I can't get old too fast; not before my son is grown. He's still just a baby."

I thought of my mother and the way her hard life had aged her, then killed her.

"You must miss him," I said, "I mean, your baby when you're out here on the road."

Her face flushed with color and pride and she winked at me and cocked her head toward the rear of the cab. I glanced over my shoulder, into the dim sleeping cabin behind the seats. There was a small crib, padded and bolted to the floor of the truck, and a baby with wispy blond curls lay with his face turned to me, sleeping so deeply and breathing so softly that I hadn't even known he was there.

Becky put a finger to her lips and shushed me before I spoke.

"Wow," I whispered, "He's right here. He's right here with you."

I stared at him, cozy in a soft blue jumper and a knitted cap, one tiny hand tucked under his cheek and the other still clutching a half-empty bottle.

"Some folks criticize me," she said, "But a momma does what she has to, if she's able."

I could have stared at the baby for hours, but I turned away from him and faced forward when I felt warm tears falling down my face.

"What's got you crying?" Becky asked me.

I didn't want to tell her, but she coaxed me.

"Sometimes when I see a baby," I whispered, "I wonder how many people will try to ruin him before he grows up."

She was silent for a moment, staring through the windshield at the highway.

"I guess the world itself will try to do that," she said, "That's why a boy needs his momma; to raise him up so he knows he's worth more than what the world will rob him of."

I was reminded of my mother again, and of the things the world had stolen from me.

"You weren't worried picking me up?" I said, "Having me in the truck with him?"

"I mostly don't take riders," she said, "But I knew you were a good kid when I saw you in the diner."

"How'd you know that?"

"Because you were polite to that bitch of a waitress," she said, "And you tipped her even though she ran you out of there."

She glanced at me and smiled.

"Besides," she said, "Now that I'm a momma, it's hard to pass up a lost boy and just leave him stranded."

I had been on the road so long, that sometimes I forgot that most people saw a kid when they looked at me. I felt aged by the weather and wizened by the wind, but if my trip through the south had taught me anything at all, it had reminded me that I was still lost.

I was on a highway headed east, back to the place I'd been born in, but I was more lost going home than I had ever been running away.

Rebecca moved me eighty miles down the road and let me off on the highway's edge, just outside of a town called Somerset. Her baby had awakened once while she drove and she let me climb in the sleeper cabin and rock him with his bottle until he fell asleep. It didn't make me believe in God, the way some people say holding a baby will, but it made me want to believe in mothers.

I climbed out onto the step-side and tossed my pack down to the grassy shoulder, but before I dropped down after it, Becky stopped me with a question.

"You got any money?"

"A few bucks," I told her, "But I'm good."

She reached across the cab, a twenty-dollar bill between her fingers, but I glanced at the baby, sleeping in his highway crib, and waved the money away. Rebecca frowned and insisted.

"He's a year and a half," she said, "He won't miss out on college, if I give you twenty dollars."

I took the bill and folded it into my shirt pocket, but I hesitated before I climbed down from the truck. I wanted to say something to her, but I had no faith in my words.

"You know about Rebecca in the Bible?" I asked her and she shook her head.

"Not really," she told me, "I'm not very Christian, I suppose."

"Neither am I," I said, "Rebecca was generous and kind, the way you are. She was a mother, too, but she had twins."

Becky's eyes widened.

"I carried twins," she said, "I lost Timmy's brother in the womb."

I didn't tell her any more of the story or that one of Rebecca's sons had grown up wicked and she spared me from the awkward moment.

"You know a lot about the Bible?" she said.

"I've read most of it," I told her, "Enough of it to make me stop believing in the rest of it."

She smiled at me, a worried mother's smile, if I had ever seen one.

"You be safe. Go home, if you're able to."

"Thanks for pickin' me up," I said, "And for letting me hold your baby. It was one of the best rides I've ever had."

I climbed down to the roadside, closed the door and smacked it twice with the palm of my hand. Rebecca blew the horn, same as when we met, and drove down the road into Somerset.

I got out on U.S. 27, heading north for Lexington. I walked for twenty minutes and caught a short ride with an old man who let me off in a town called Eubank.

When he drove away, I noticed a sticker on the rear bumper of his truck

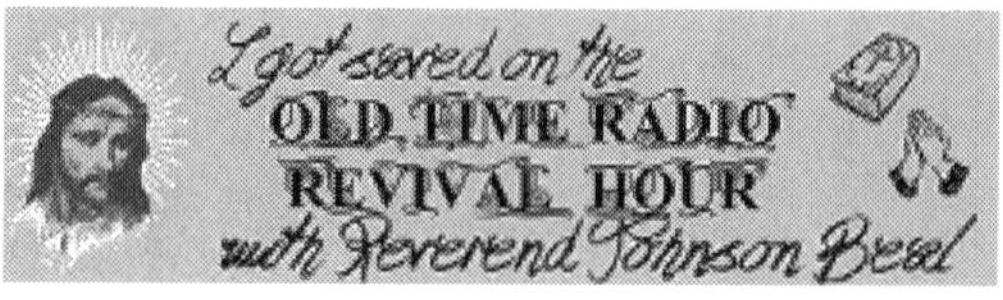

THREE
BLIND BOY BLUES

Eubank was a spot on the road, really; a town of less than four hundred people that straddled two counties and didn't promise much traffic. I walked through town to Main Street, looking for a café or a burger stand, thinking I had made a mistake cutting north back at Somerset,.

On a corner in what passed as downtown Eubank, I heard a teasing cackle and saw a crow up on a streetlight.

Go away, bird; I haven't seen Lonnie James since Memphis.

The sidewalk wasn't crowded, but there were people out, window shopping in the afternoon sun or resting on benches. Two teenaged girls pointed me to a hamburger stand, where a greasy-haired kid in a white paper cap took my order.

"I'll have the burger special," I said, glancing up at a chalkboard menu that promised a burger, fries and soda for two and a half bucks.

"Hamburger or cheeseburger?" the kid asked, scribbling on a green order pad.

"What's the difference?"

He blinked at me.

"Cheese," he said, "Cheeseburger's got cheese on it."

"I meant the price," I said, "How much more for the cheeseburger?"

I paid the ten cents extra for a slice of melting cheese on my burger and ate at the counter, under a whirring fan, listening to Tom Petty and the Heartbreakers on the jukebox. The kid in the paper hat pretended to be busy wiping the counter, but his curiosity got the better of him and he tossed his towel in a bucket and came and leaned on the counter in front of me.

"I seen you leave that pack outside," he said, "You a hitchhiker?"

I swallowed a mouthful of greasy burger and soggy bun.

"Yeah," I told him, "Just passin' through north."

He nodded and hitched his thumbs through the drawstring on his apron.

"I thought so," he said, "You might as well walk on outta Eubank. There ain't much traffic through here and most folks won't pick up a stranger."

I agreed that I would probably be walking out when I left town and asked him if there was a park nearby where I could rest, maybe even sleep over night.

"I wouldn't go sleepin' in the park, if I was you," he said, "Cops wouldn't go for that at all. They ain't too welcoming to outsiders...if they got a low look about 'em."

I grinned and shook my head.

"Oh, I ain't sayin' I think you got a low look," he explained, "Not at all. I'm tellin' you how a cop might look at you."

He refilled my soda for free and I took it with me when I left. I walked a couple blocks and found the park the kid had warned me against sleeping in and settled down on my pack in the grass just off the sidewalk.

I smoked cigarettes and wished I had some pot, but Roselyn had left me dry, not just broke. The day was bright, even with sunglasses on, but it felt good to laze in the sun after a week of recurring rain. I propped my half-empty soda cup in the lush grass and found one of my harmonicas hiding in a jacket pocket and the other in the top flap of my pack.

I passed the time playing what I knew and trying out new riffs and turnarounds and the girls I had met downtown came along and stood on the sidewalk. They giggled and blushed while I played and clapped their hands when I tried to impress them with the sound of a long, lonesome train.

I faked a passable version of Springsteen's "Factory" and in the middle of that mournful tune, a woman passing by on the sidewalk paused to listen. She stooped and dropped a handful of coins into the burger joint cup at my feet, splashing lemon-lime soda on my boots, and laughed when she realized her mistake.

"Well, go on an' keep it," she said as she turned away, "Since I ruined your soda."

I grinned and the two girls giggled and we all glanced out at the street, where a black and white patrol car cruised slowly past the park. A cop leaned out the window and stared at me, turned the car around at the end of the block and came back for a second look.

He parked the car along the curb and climbed out, adjusted his wide leather belt and walked toward me with one hand tipping the brim of his cap and the other one resting on the butt of his revolver. He gave the girls a glance as he passed them and they stepped back a few feet, but didn't leave, and he stopped on the grass right in front of me and hunkered down to stare at my face.

I didn't say anything, but I stopped playing the blues and slipped my harmonica into my shirt pocket. The cop waved one hand close in front of my face and I flinched.

"I knew you wasn't blind," he grumbled.

Blind?

He stood up with his hands at his hips, one still on his sidearm and the other on his baton, and stepped backwards onto the sidewalk.

"I'm gonna need you to stand up, son," he said, "Clasp your hands atop your head, stand up and turn around with your back to me."

I sighed and started to rise and one of the girls protested.

"What's he doin' wrong?"

"Yeah," the other one said, "He ain't doin' anything wrong, but playin' music."

I got to my feet and turned away from them, my fingers interlocked in my hair, and I heard the cop scold the girls, to scare them away.

"You kids get on home," he said, "Before I start to wonderin' what you're doin' hangin' 'round the park with a vagrant."

A vagrant?

I heard shuffling footsteps on the sidewalk as the girls made their escape and then the cop was standing behind me. With one hand, he covered my own and with the other, he slipped my knife from its sheath. He searched me, skimming his hand down my back and under my arms, and hooked his fingers under my belt to feel along my waist and I thought of The Troll-Man.

Just lemme get it in my mouth.

I heard him slip his handcuffs from his belt and he pulled my left arm forcefully behind me, twisting it against the small of my back.

"What laws am I breaking?"

One cuff clicked tight around my wrist. The cop pulled my other hand from the top of my head, the other cuff clicked, and he spun me around to face him.

"Well, you're panhandlin' an' that's only an infraction," he said.

I shook my head.

"That's wrong, Officer. I wasn't panhandling or begging for money at all."

He glanced down at my cup of soda and stared at the coins beneath the bubbles. I sighed.

"Now, pretendin' to be blind so's folks give you money," he said, "That could work out to fraud, if the judge thinks it's so."

I almost cursed, but I kept my temper with the cop.

"What makes you think I'm faking bein' blind?"

He frowned and gave me a slight shove toward his patrol car.

"You can see, cant'cha?" he drawled.

"I mean, why do you think I'm doin' it," I said, "I never told anybody I was blind. I hardly even talked to anyone at all."

He put one hand on my head again and the other on my shoulder and pressed me into the back seat of his cruiser.

"You're wearin' sunglasses," he said. He slammed the door, locked my duffel bag in the trunk and climbed into the driver's seat. He mumbled into the microphone of the car radio and glanced at me in the rearview mirror.

"You're wearing sunglasses, too," I said.

His grin barely passed for a frown.

"I ain't playin' any harmonica," he said, "And I ain't some homeless, white-trash queer."

FOUR
LAWS AND ORDERS

"You and me both know why you got hauled in, so why don't we just cut past the bullshit here?"

There were only two cops at the police station and I had a feeling they were the only cops in the entire town. The one who brought me in was busy searching through my gear, everything dumped out of my duffel onto a long table and the bag turned inside out. He had unrolled and shaken out my blankets, done the same to my tent and was searching all of my clothes, making an even bigger mess of them than Roselyn had done.

The other cop was older and the stripes on his uniform sleeves put him in charge. He seemed bored with my arrest and I could tell he knew I wasn't a criminal, but he also seemed determined to lock me up, if only to satisfy his contempt for me.

"*All* of it's bullshit," I said, "Him grabbin' me up is bullshit and it's bullshit that I'm even sitting here at all, still cuffed."

The cop had been slouched back in his chair with his arms crossed over his chest, but he leaned forward, reached across the desk and took the box of Pall Malls from my breast pocket. He shook one loose, planted it between his lips and slipped the pack back into my shirt. He wore a slim smirk when he leaned back again, struck a match to the cigarette and blew smoke in my face.

"Now, that's where you're wrong, son," he said, "So let's do like I said and just cut through what's bullshit and what ain't."

I didn't answer back.

"I can't put you up before the judge on Denny's charges," he said, "Panhandlin' is an infraction, not a crime, and that business about you posin' as blind: well, that's dumb, but funny as hell."

It may have been funny to him, but I didn't get the joke, even though I knew I was about to become the punchline.

"Now, here's the truth of it all," he said, still sucking on the cigarette he had stolen from me, "What I *can* charge you with is loitering and resisting an officer, if I want to..."

"I didn't resist."

The cop glanced across the room at his partner.

"Hey, Denny," he said, "Didn't you say you were gonna put in your report that this boy resisted you?"

Denny looked up from rummaging through my clothes and stared at his boss. He looked confused, but then his dim eyes brightened just a bit and he nodded.

"Sure did. I had to just about yank his arm around just to cuff him."

The sergeant looked back at me and smiled, but it only made him look like the kind of man who likes the taste of bullshit, as long as it's his own he's chewing.

"You got a cocky way," he said, "And a look about you that says you think you're smarter than everybody else, but interrupt me again, son, and you'll be sorry for it."

I nodded.

"Now, Officer Dennison is lookin' through your things there and if he finds any dope in 'em, I'm gonna charge you with possession."

I had been angry that Roselyn had stolen my pot along with my money, but it turned out that part of her thievery had been a kind of favor. I remembered the motel housekeeper, Ardith, and the things she had said about the Lord's mysterious ways.

The cop blew another cloud of smoke in my face and stubbed the cigarette out in an ashtray shaped like a badge.

"I can also hold you until we're sure you're really who you say you are and you ain't wanted in some other county or state. *That's* what I'm inclined to do, and you could walk on out of here tomorrow or the day after that, so long as your name runs clean."

He took a shot of coffee from a mug with his own portrait on it and grimaced.

"Denny never could make coffee worth a shit."

He leaned over the desk again, but he didn't take my cigarettes or reach for me at all; he crossed his hands on the desk and stared at me with eyes so hard they looked out of place in his soft face.

"You ain't welcome around here," he said and I thought of Miss Millie and how right she had been.

You're as welcome here as you feel.

"You're trash and trouble," he drawled, "Even if you ain't a bad one, trouble follows folks like you around and I ain't havin' it in Eubank."

I nodded again, but I didn't interrupt him. I knew I didn't have any warrants and he would have to let me go once he had proof of my name, so I went along with him and didn't argue over being locked up.

I'll get a shower and a few meals out of it.

"The condition of your release, of course, bein' that you don't ever come back around here," he said, "If you ever do, I'll find a reason to put you away...or make one up."

He flashed his wolfish grin.

"You see, son, there's law and order...and then there's laws and orders."

Dennison finally let me out of the handcuffs. He took me into another room, photographed me and pressed my fingertips onto an ink pad, then a card with ten blank squares. He left identifying smudges in nine of the squares then stared at my hands.

"Hold up your fingers," he said.

I held my hands out in front of me and wiggled all nine of my fingers. I had been born with only one thumb, but Denny seemed to be figuring some complicated mathematics to work out which digit was missing.

"Your thumb," he said, "What happened to it?"

"Born that way."

"Kinda funny," he said, "A hitchhiker who ain't got a thumb."

"It only takes one," I said.

He poked his head out the door and hollered at the sergeant.

"Hey, Carl! What do I do if he only has nine fingers instead of all ten? About the empty square, I mean?"

I heard the sergeant sigh then holler back.

"Leave it blank, dummy!"

Denny came back to the counter and gave me a paper towel to wipe the ink off my fingers. He stared at the fingerprint card and frowned, as if he were unhappy about leaving one of the boxes blank. I pointed at the card and tried to make him feel better about it.

"There's a space there to write down all my scars and deformities."

FIVE

LINCOLN COUNTY TIME

The police station housed a small jail and Dennison took me through a steel door and down a short hallway that was lined on either side with a pair of cells. Three of the cells were empty and the fourth held a man in his late forties, wearing wire-framed glasses and a loose orange jumpsuit. He had been lying down, reading a thick book, but he sat up on the edge of his bunk and stared at us.

"Don't lock him in here with me," he said to Dennison, "The concierge assured me I would have a private room."

The cop sighed and jangled a brass keyring loose from his belt.

"I wouldn't lock any kid up with the likes o' you, William Axton Junior," he said, "He's got trouble enough without talkin' up a fiend like you."

Dennison jammed a big key into the lock of the next cell, turned it with a clank and rolled the gate open. He gave me a little shove into the cage and locked me up, exactly as he had meant to the moment he saw me in the park, playing harmonica for two local girls. He turned and left out the steel door and William Axton called out after him as he went.

"You do know we can talk each other up just fine through the bars, don't you?"

The door slammed and we were left together in the dim jail, staring at each other across the hallway. I was still wearing my own clothing, the same jeans and flannel I'd had on when I was arrested, and the jumpsuit Axton was wearing, stamped INMATE and L.C.C.C. in bold block lettering, meant he was doing county time and probably wouldn't go walking free in a matter of days, the way I would.

He had a bony face and thin, longish hair that swept back from his forehead and hung down his neck in a short ponytail. Everyone looks like a criminal when they're dressed-out in a jailhouse jumpsuit and I wondered what kind of clothes he might wear if he were free out on the streets. I sat on my bunk, looking at him sitting on his, and imagined him dressed in chinos, a clean blue work shirt and hiking boots. He looked like a teacher, but the kind who smokes pot and doesn't teach down to his students.

Dennison had confiscated my Zippo and the open pack of Pall Malls from my shirt pocket, but he let me keep a sealed pack and gave me a book of matches. I leaned back on the thin mat that would be my bed and smoked. William Axton got up from his bunk and stood at the bars.

"I don't suppose you might spare me one of those cigarettes?" he said, "I'll give you my brownie when supper comes around, if you want it."

I shook one loose and tossed it to him. It fell short, but rolled close enough to his cell that he was able to stoop and snatch it from the floor. He stood up with it jammed between his lips and shrugged.

"Toss me over that pack of matches? I promise I'll toss 'em back to you."

I never liked wasting a match, especially in jail, and something about him promising to toss them back to me made me wonder if he would. I got up and stood at the edge of my cell, stretched my arm through the bars and held my lit cigarette out toward him.

"Jump start it."

He stretched his own arm through the bars and was able to just touch the tip of his cigarette to mine. It flared the faintest orange and he jerked it back quickly, stuffed it in his mouth and puffed on it until it caught. He took a deep pull and exhaled with a satisfied sigh.

"I thank you," he said, "And I wonder what it is you stand accused of."

I stared at him and smoked.

"I'm accused of being blind."

His eyebrows arched and the corners of his smile followed.

"Clearly, you're not blind."

I shrugged.

"No," I said, "I'm innocent of it."

I didn't ask him what he stood accused of. I had learned on the road, and in a few other jails, that most men don't like being asked what they've done, if it's something they aren't proud of. We didn't speak for the rest of the afternoon, but when supper came that evening, he offered me his brownie and I took it to put away for later.

When our empty trays were taken away, he went back to his reading and I stretched out on my bunk with a smoke. He didn't ask to bum another and I was glad, because I wouldn't have given it to him so soon after the last and if he wanted one later, I would make him promise me his coffee at breakfast.

The county issue mattress was hardly more than a thin, rough pad laid out on a hard steel frame, but it was softer than most of the places I had slept over the last three and a half years and I fell asleep remembering Miss Millie.

You don't look so used to sleepin' in tall comfort.

I was running down a dry, dirt track, through the shadows of bare, twisted trees, toward a church in the distance, cast against a dead, grey sunset in stark silhouette. I knew I was caught in a dream because the faster I ran, the farther away from the church I seemed and the road stretched out before me like an endless thread.

A storm ran riot all around me, not locusts or even dust, but a rain of dried, dead flowers that fell grey as moths from the sky. They drifted on the wind and piled up on the ground, their crisp petals crunching beneath my boots as I ran from a great, roaring beast, long and deadly and black.

Run...run...run.

The car was close behind me, lurching through the dust of dead flowers and I didn't look back to see who was driving it. I would find out soon enough, once it caught up to me, if it was my mother, Elvis Presley or some other ghost.

I reached the barren churchyard, littered with fallen petals, and I recognized the church house and the garden of gravestones beyond it. It was Calvin Thomas' chapel in Arkansas, where I had been welcomed and safe once before, and I ran through the downpour of daisies, up the steps and into the church and was caught in a long, dark box.

A soft, velvet darkness lay against my face and I knew that I was in a coffin, dead and dreaming of life. I couldn't feel my heartbeat or if I was even breathing, but I knew my eyes were open to the dark. I pressed my hands against the shadows and a stream of light crept in, so I knew I hadn't been blinded by my death. I forced the casket open, sat up on my deathbed and knew the fear of a dead man who had denied the existence of God.

I was wearing my ragged road clothes and the tie I had borrowed from Sneaks, but my wrists were bound in handcuffs and my feet were shackled in chains.

The church was crowded with mourners, every pew filled with veiled, weeping shadows, but my eyes were drawn to the pulpit, where Elvis Presley led a purple-robed choir, shaking his hips and thrusting his pelvis, a bible held open in one hand and a dead raven dangling by its talons from the other.

They were singing some dark hymn I'd never heard, but I recognized it quickly as the devil's lullaby; a song to send a boy to hell by, one of endless, dreamless sleep. The choir was a single, dread voice, made whole by many voices, every one of them a bottomless bass or a dark baritone. Elvis sang above them, against them, below them, his tenor too earthly and pure for their dark harmony. The song had a painful melody and the chorus was a guttural prayer, but they ended it together as one on a note like a hiss. The mourners rattled up from the pews for a standing ovation, the choir spread their hands to heaven and the ghost of Elvis bowed and flourished his cape.

"Dearly beloved," he said in his silken drawl, "We gather here today to celebrate the death of a very bad boy, who ran away and never went home."

The choir hung their heads in sorrow and the mourners sighed together like a grove of whispering trees. Still bound in my coffin, I stared at Elvis and he slipped me a sideways grin and a slow, sly wink.

"Even the King of Rock and Roll knows a good boy always listens to his mama," he preached, "And he always comes quick when she calls him home."

The mourners erupted in hallelujah and I turned to face them, to see who had gathered to pay their respects to a boy who had left behind no one. All of them were women, not a single man among them, and they reached up all at once and pulled back their veils.

Every single one of them had my mother's face.

"You should have gone home," they sighed, "You should have gone home, you should have gone home, you should have..."

At the back of the hall, behind the last row of pews, the church door burst open. The sun rushed into the hall, spoiling my dark funeral with light and Miss Millie stepped over the threshold with angels behind her.

"Get out of this house!' she shouted, "Get out in the name of the living God and leave this here poor boy alone."

The mourners shrieked a collective curse and fled the church like dark wisps through the rafters. The choir all dropped dead in their robes and Elvis left the building.

I stared at Miss Millie and she stared straight back and graced me with her gentle smile.

"Hurry," she said, "God ain't give up on you yet, but He's gettin' a might impatient."

I asked her what I should do; if I should go home or stay forgotten, but she only smiled until she was gone, as if she hadn't been there at all.

I rose from the coffin, no longer bound, and ran up the aisle and out of the church. I rushed through the doorway, down the steps and to the road, where the long black car I had run from sat waiting to carry me home. The passenger door hung open and I climbed into the car beside my mother. Her hands rested on the steering wheel, clothed in black gloves, and she wore a mourner's veil across her face.

"Drive, Momma," I said, "I knew I couldn't run away forever."

She reached one gloved hand to her face and pulled back the veil. It wasn't my mother, after all.

"Where's your fuckin' milk jug, boy?"

The Troll-Man was driving the car.

I screamed and screamed until...

I woke up in the jail cell, bolting straight up in my bunk. The jail was darker now than it had been when I fell asleep, but I could see the dim shape of William Axton, standing at the bars of his cell, staring across the hall into my eyes.

"Did I scream?"

"Oh, you screamed," he whispered, cocking his head toward the steel door that separated us from our jailers "You sure *did* fucking scream."

"Bad dreams," I whispered back.

I lit two cigarettes on one match and tossed one of them across the hallway to William Axton. He caught it in a flurry of sparks and ashes and settled down on the floor to smoke. I told him about the storms and the phantom car that stalked me; about Elvis, my mother and The Troll-Man, too.

When I finished, I lit another smoke and offered one to him, but he declined it. He went to his bunk and brought his thick book back to the bars. He began to read aloud and I knew that he was reading from The Bible.

"As I looked, behold, a storm wind was coming from the north, a great cloud with fire flashing forth continually and a bright light around it, and in its midst something like glowing metal in the midst of the fire. Within it there were figures resembling four living beings."

He took a breath.

"And this was their appearance: they had human form. Each of them had four faces and four wings."

He closed the book and held it against his chest.

"The Bible says we dream," he said, "But it also says we dream visions."

I shook my head and pulled on my cigarette.

"I don't believe in any of that," I said, "Besides, you read about four figures, but in my dreams, there are only three. The Troll-Man, my mother and Elvis."

He grinned and changed his mind about the cigarette.

"Three that you've seen," he whispered, "But maybe there are dreams and visions yet to come."

He went back to his bunk and soon fell asleep, but I stayed awake and remembered a fourth figure that I had forgotten. The very first time I had dreamed of the car, I hadn't seen the driver's face; just a shadowy form in the driver's seat, blurred by a storm of dry dust.

SIX
COFFEE AND SMOKES

In the morning, it was cold in the cellblock and I woke up early and pissed into a stainless-steel toilet with my back to William Axton. He was awake, but still in his bunk, with his blanket pulled up to his neck and his Bible open in front of his face. I washed my face in a dingy basin, dried it on a coarse towel and lit a cigarette. The flare of the match in the early dark caught Axton's attention.

"Might I beg just one more of those?" he said, "I do love a cigarette in the morning."

I scowled at him. I had never been talkative in the morning and I almost always woke up grouchy if the night had been a bad one of dreaming. I had been generous with my smokes the night before because Axton had sat and talked with me after I woke up screaming, but that morning I wasn't giving anything away for free.

"If you want one, you gotta trade your coffee for it."

He frowned.

"I meant to save the smoke to accompany my coffee," he said, "Now, neither will be as good without the other."

I counted the cigarettes left in the pack. I wasn't feeling any more generous than I had been a moment before, but I understood his point about pairing his smoke and coffee.

"Tell you what," I said, "I'll give you two cigarettes and you can save one back for tomorrow morning's coffee."

He thought it over.

"Tomorrow I'll be back at the county jail. I'm only down here for a court date on a local matter, then it's straight back up the county."

He sighed, took his glasses off his face and cleaned them on the sleeve of his jumpsuit.

"Of course, once they find me guilty and sentence me," he said, "I'll stop winding my watch on Lincoln County time and they'll send me up the state to the penitentiary."

I glared across the hallway, bored with all of his talk about jails and prison. He was the kind of man who doesn't get along so well behind bars; he talked too much and he was nosy, too. He seemed to be inviting me to ask him what he had done to wind up prison-bound, but I didn't ask and I didn't care.

"You got a fuckin' point?" I said, "What's it matter anyway, which jail you're in for your damned coffee and smoke?"

He smiled, but it wasn't friendly. It was the kind of smile you mostly see on a man who's too small for all his arrogance.

"The point, my young wandering friend," he said, "Is that the coffee up in county is shit, as is the food. Here, our trays are filled at the local cafe, not ladled with slop from a jailhouse chef."

I sighed.

"You gonna trade the coffee or not?"

"I'll trade it for the two cigarettes," he said, "If you're willing to sweeten the deal. Before they come to let you outta here today, let me have that pack of matches you've been hording."

I wouldn't need the matches once I was free. I'd have my Zippo back, and the matches I had stashed in my gear. If it got me a second cup of coffee and shut William Axton up for a while, he could have the damned matches.

I tossed him a lit cigarette.

"You get the second one after I get the coffee," I said, "No offense."

"None taken," he grinned, "We are, after all, a criminal and a low man of the highway."

Dennison brought our breakfast. I wondered if he ever slept or went home or was he always on duty, hanging around the police station or patrolling in his cruiser, protecting Eubank's teenage girls from low men of the highway. He passed a tray through a slot in the bars, hotcakes and scrambled eggs with sausage and coffee, too.

"Pass me Axton's coffee, too," I said, "He traded it away to me for a cigarette."

Dennison smirked at me and glanced into the other cell, but he handed me the steaming cup from Axton's tray.

"Best drink it up quick," he said, "I'm comin' back in fifteen minutes to let you out. We got the word back on you."

He passed Axton his breakfast and went to the steel door, but he turned around and nodded at me.

"You ain't wanted by the law anywhere," he said, "But you ain't exactly clean."

He left out the door and William Axton shook his head in contempt.

"I can't stand that ignorant way of speaking that passes for homey charm around here."

"What were you?" I said, "Before you got locked up?"

"I'm a poet," he said, "Unpublished, mind you."

I didn't ask him about his poetry. If he wrote anything like he spoke, all his rhymes would be pretentious and predictable. I had the first cup of coffee with my pancakes and the second with a cigarette and tossed Axton the matches and another Pall Mall.

Dennison came back and opened my cell and nudged me along the hall, as if he thought I needed encouragement to leave his jail. William Axton called out to me as I went.

"When you gonna stop runnin' away from God?"

"I'm not runnin' from any god," I said, "I'm just staying away from the world."

I passed his cell and waited at the doorway while Dennison fumbled with his keyring.

"If you're runnin' away from the world," Axton said, "You're runnin' away from God."

I turned around to look at him.

"God needs low men, too," he grinned, "For doing His dirty work."

"That's not from the Bible."

"No," he said, "That's from the Gospel of William Axton Junior."

He winked and Dennison shoved me through the door and locked it behind us.

"Crazy fiend," he mumbled under his breath.

SEVEN
I SHALL BE RELEASED

The sergeant wasn't in the office. My duffel bag leaned against the wall, waiting for me to take it back to the road, but Dennison sat me in a chair and brought my release papers from a stack on the sergeant's desk.

"Sign these," he grunted, "Carl said to give you a ride up to the Garrard County line and get you started down the road a-ways."

"I'll pass on the ride," I told him, "I've been in the back of your car one time too many already."

Dennison smirked.

"It ain't negotiable."

Outside, at the curb, Dennison slammed my gear into the trunk of his patrol car. He handed me a plastic bag that held my wallet, the harmonica I'd been playing in the park and the open pack of Pall Malls.

"What about my lighter?" I said, "And my knife."

"Don't worry 'bout it," he grumbled, "You'll get everything back when I let you out."

He stepped up onto the sidewalk and slipped his handcuffs from his belt as he came toward me. I stepped back from him.

"I'm not letting you put those on me."

"You gotta wear 'em in the car," he said, "Just 'cause you ain't wanted, that don't mean you can't be dangerous."

I shook my head and kept three feet between us. If he wanted to restrain me, he would have to find a reason to arrest me again.

"Dennison...I just came out of your jail. You know I'm not armed, and there's a steel mesh between the front seat and the back."

He frowned at my use of his name and took another step toward me.

"I'm not under arrest anymore," I said, "So give me my gear or give me a ride, but you're not putting those fucking cuffs on me."

He drove me up the highway and a few miles out of town, Dennison seemed to get over losing our argument over the handcuffs. He relaxed behind the wheel, found a country music station on the radio and glanced at me in the rearview mirror.

"How old are you anyway?" he said.

"You wrote down my date of birth about a dozen times," I said, "And you don't know how old I am?"

In the mirror, I saw him furrow his brow and blink and he looked his own age for the first time since I had seen him. Officer Dennison looked less than ten years older than I was, still growing out of being a boy, but wearing a badge and a gun that belonged on a man.

"Shit, I know," he said, "I forget it, but I know you're of age or we woulda sent you up the county to the juvenile detention."

I sighed.

"I'm twenty," I said.

He glanced at me again and the boy was gone from the mirror. All I saw was a cop too dumb for his job and too much of a bully to keep any peace.

"Why the hell you fuckin' around out on the road then?" he said, "Instead o' tryin' to be something?"

I stared at the back of his head.

"It's none of your fucking business," I said, "And it's not against the law."

"You ain't gotta get obnoxious about it," he said, "I'm just sayin' you could stop ramblin' from one town to the other and settle in one of 'em."

I almost laughed.

"Just not in Eubank, Kentucky," I said.

"We got a right to keep trouble off our own streets," he said, "You ain't our kind is all, but you ain't as bad as that fiend William Axton, and he comes from right in town."

"What did he do, anyway?" I said.

Dennison stared at me in the mirror.

"He killed his own mother," he said, "Set her trailer on fire one night and burned her up in her sleep."

Jesus fucking Christ.

I didn't feel like talking any more just then, but I reminded myself to tell Dennison that William Axton Junior had a pack of matches in his cell.

We passed a sign that marked the county line and Dennison pulled the cruiser off the highway. He let me out of the car and hauled my pack out of the trunk. He tossed it in the dirt at my feet.

"Your knife's in the duffel," he said, "Zippo's in there somewheres, too."

I hunkered down and opened the flaps of my pack, but Dennison didn't get back in the car.

"Carl said to remind you that you ain't welcome ever comin' back to Eubank."

I glanced up at him, squinting against the glare of the sun.

"I think I got the message when he told me himself," I said.

"All the same..."

He yanked a long black flashlight from a loop on his belt, raised it up and brought it down across the side of my head, just above my left ear. He held back some, but he struck me hard enough that the world flashed white and I went to my hands and knees in the dirt. I could feel a hard knot already raising on my skull and the pain of it was violent.

I got to my knees, but not my feet. I was dizzy and nearly deaf beneath the ringing in my ears. My hand went to my hip, but my knife wasn't there. If it had been, I would have been shot and killed on the side of the road.

God ain't give up on you yet, but he's gettin' a might impatient.

"You're a real sonofabitch, Denny."

"You want another one?" he said.

I stared up at him and I knew the only way I had of fighting him back was to stay down and let him hit me again.

"Go ahead..."

That time he split my forehead open and left me in the dirt. He climbed back into the car, turned it around on the highway and pointed it back toward Eubank.

He could go to hell and William Axton Junior, fire starter and mother-killing fiend, could smuggle his matches all the way up to the county jail, for all I cared.

EIGHT
REVELATION

I used a bandana to stop the bleeding, but I knew without seeing my reflection that my forehead was bruised worse than it was cracked open and the skin around my left eye was going black on its way to purple. The scratches and bruises left by The Troll-Man hadn't healed over yet, either, and I wondered how I'd ever catch a ride, lurching along the highway like a battered bogeyman.

I walked for miles, sometimes stumbling in the weeds on the highway's edge, but I hurried past a crow spying from a fencepost and nearly ran when another shrieked at me from a power line. I saw two more on the wing and remembered what Lonnie James had said about the birds.

They know carrion when they see it.

I wondered if they were hunting me, too, now.

I walked straight out of the morning and into the afternoon, resting from time to time in shady spots along the highway, and by the earliest part of the evening, I had walked a third of the way to Lexington. My face had swollen up around my eye, squeezing it almost completely closed, and the thin gash on my forehead had opened up again and started to bleed. I was tired and my head was buzzing with dull pain that was sharper when I touched my wounds and I made up my mind that I would get off the road and pitch my tent beside the next running stream I came across.

At a wide curve in the road, I dug my canteen out of my pack, had two long swallows of cool water and trickled some over my head and face. I pushed my damp hair back, gently, from my pulsing forehead and hardly noticed more than a shifting shadow when a brand-new Cadillac pulled over in the breakdown lane just ahead of me.

I thought I heard a raven shout, but it was only the driver honking the Cadillac's horn. I screwed the cap on my canteen and stowed it in my pack as I hurried up the highway beneath the lowering sun. The car was shiny and lean, with whitewall tires and curved fins, and I caught my reflection in its dark tinted windows, as I came along the passenger's side. I stared at my battered face and thought of Luanna.

Honey, you're about as scruffy lookin' as a badger on a bender.

The car had been waxed smooth and shiny and it sparkled like a great black diamond on the edge of the road. I couldn't see in through the tint, but the passenger window lowered with an electric hum as I reached for the chrome door handle.

The car was as immaculate on the inside as it was on its skin, a finely engineered luxury, made somewhat homey by tokens of family and faith; a bible on the seat and photographs of two young children and a kind-faced woman taped to the dashboard display. The car was driven by a rail thin man wearing an expensive black suit and a felt fedora. He was leaning across the leather bench seat, his left hand on the steering wheel and his right one resting on the Bible.

"Sweet mercy, boy," he said, "What happened to your face?"

His voice was vaguely familiar. It reminded me of someone I had met, but I couldn't remember who it had been through the buzzing in my head. I stared into the car, but my vision was clouding over and I couldn't see the driver's face clearly. I felt dizzy from staring at him.

"I got beat up," I said, "I don't feel very good, mister."

He got out of the Cadillac and came around quickly, his shiny shoes flapping on the warmed-over blacktop.

He's wearing his squeaks.

The man wrapped one arm around my shoulders, pulled the car door open and helped me inside. He eased me onto the seat, strapped the seatbelt around my waist and gently shut the door. I stared at the photographs of his wife and children as he hurried around the front of the car and by the time he slid in behind the wheel, I was fading away.

"Who was it that beat you up?" he said, "The roads are thick with thieves."

I still couldn't place his voice.

"A cop did it," I said, "Dennison did it."

I heard him gasp.

"A cop?" he said, "But why? Why did he do it to you?"

I felt weightless against the leather seat.

"Because I wasn't blind."

I didn't say anything else. I couldn't.

We drove with the windows down and the breeze felt peaceful on my bruises. The highway slithered beneath the car and soothed me toward a slippery sleep. The radio was tuned to an AM station that gave equal time to God and crops, and I fell asleep to a weather report and the sound of the Cadillac's driver mumbling a prayer; something about temptation and the blood of Christ.

I dreamed the road beneath the Cadillac's wheels had gone to ruin and the clear, blue sky above it gone to dust. The driver tipped his hat and revealed small horns beneath its brim and when he smiled, his long, forked tongue fell from his mouth like a two-headed snake. I knew who he was; I'd known all along, and I woke up from the nightmare to a vision come to pass.

The throbbing buzz in my skull remained, but my vision had cleared and I stared across the seat at the devil behind the wheel. He had no horns or serpent tongue, but his face was drawn and darkened by a grin of guilt and glee. His trousers lay open, pushed down around his thighs and his skin was pale and hairless. His left hand gripped the steering wheel and his right one was wrapped around his stiffened penis like a bony claw, a twenty-dollar bill folded between his fingers. He had a tattoo on his pelvis; a small black cross wrapped in thorny barbed-wire.

We had left the smooth asphalt of the highway and were going too fast down a rough dirt road. Thick trees flashed by on either side and a dust cloud rose around us and blew in through the open windows.

LOCUSTS!

The driver leered at me and let go of himself long enough to wave the twenty-dollar bill in my face.

"I bet a boy like you gets hungry," he whispered, "Goin' down the road all lean and tempting."

I pushed his hand away and tried to stretch across the seat to hit him, but the seatbelt held me tight and he slapped me across the searing bruise on the side of my face. A sea of stars exploded behind my eyes and I reached for my lap with both hands and struggled with the seatbelt buckle's release. My pants had been opened, too.

The seatbelt clicked and I was free and I lunged across the seat with both fists flying. I hit him twice on the right side of his face and his head banged hard against the doorframe. The Cadillac lurched and rocketed forward then slid to a sideways stop in the middle of the road, spraying even more dust into the air and in through the windows.

It's not a storm; it's a swarm.

The driver twisted in his seat, one hand held up against my blows and the other bent behind him, fumbling for the door handle. I hit him in his mouth and he hollered at me, spraying blood from his lips.

"It's your fault!" he screamed, "You brung the devil right into my car!"

I knew that raging, accusing scream and I had no doubt about where I had heard it before. It was the slick, dark voice that had filled the cab of Dalton Cummings rig, spitting sin and salvation right through cheap stereo speakers. His free hand found my bruises again and his other hand found the latch and pushed the car door open behind him. He tumbled into the dirt and I rushed out after him, chasing his sobs and screams into the dusty daylight.

He lay on his back, spread wide open before me and I kicked him in his ribs and stomped on one of his hands. He filled his palm with a handful of road dust and tossed it into my eyes, but I leaned into him, swung blindly for his face and found it.

"No!" he screamed, "Stop before you kill me."

I stood over him, my head pulsing and my forehead bleeding again, and he stared up at me, one hand held out shaking in front of his face.

"You foolish fucking boy," he hissed, "You'll pay so dearly for this."

I kicked him again with a steel-toed boot and the air whooshed out of his lungs.

"Say one more word," I shouted, "Say just one and I'll cut you open."

His eyes narrowed into slits and his bloody mouth opened again.

"God sees you!"

I bent over him and knocked his head back into the dirt. I grabbed a handful of shirt and suspenders and yanked him toward my fist, hitting him once, twice, again and again.

The dust had settled around us and the air was clear and still. The only sound was the buzzing in my head as I beat the preacher bloody. He cried out every time I struck him, but he spit out blood and teeth instead of words.

The shadow of a cross lay long across the road and I remembered the last words William Axton had spoken to me as I walked out of the Eubank jail.

God needs low men, too, for doing His dirty work.

I found my feet and wiped blood and dust from my face with the sleeve of my shirt. I spit into the dirt and wrapped my hand around the pommel of my knife. The blade hissed slipping out of the leather and gleamed in the faded sunlight. If God had brought me there to kill a man like Johnson Beal, then He was a god I could believe in, after all.

"You're no different than The Troll-Man," I said, "Only your fingernails are cleaner."

Johnson Beal lay sprawled in the dirt, his expensive pants wrinkled down around his knees, and his shirt ripped open at his throat. He stared at the long steel blade in my hands and his mouth stretched sideways in a begging whisper.

"Please don't kill me."

I leaned forward and another shadow fell over us both, a dark and sinister shape descending upon the cross. I glanced into the sky and my blind eye closed to heaven's glare, but my good eye showed me clearly that the devil had found me, too.

A great bird as black as hell settled at the top of a telephone pole, stretched its neck and cocked its head at the bloody business below. It cackled with murderous mischief, a heckler and a rabble-rouser in a feathered cloak.

God was there, but so was the devil, and I was too faithless to know which one of them was the witness and which was my accomplice. I felt warm blood trickling down my forehead and hot tears running down my face and I hunched over the preacher and put the thin edge of my knife against his throat.

On the wind or in my head, I heard Miss Millie's voice, as clear as a prayer.

God ain't give up on you yet.

Beal's eyes were wide circles of fear in the swollen mess I had made of his face and his mouth was a gaping pit of silent accusation.

I pressed the knife into his flesh, drew tiny droplets of blood and Beal sucked down a breath that might have been his last. I held him by the silk of his shirt and spit into his face.

"If I knew which of them wanted me to kill you," I hissed, "I'd do it right here and now."

I rose up and kicked him once more and as soon as my knife was sheathed at my hip, he scrambled away from me in the dirt. His billfold had come out of his pocket and lay open on the road, a thick spread of bills poking out of its folds. I stooped and picked it up and the preacher rose up from the ground as far as his knees.

Now that he hadn't been murdered, some of his righteousness had returned and he spoke in a threatening hiss.

"You don't wanna rob me, boy," he said, "You have no idea who you're foolin' with."

I took his driver's license out of his wallet and stared at it, just to be sure of what I already knew.

"I know who you are," I said, "I heard you on the radio; sending everybody to hell and stealing their money."

He sneered at me and pushed his sweaty hair out of his eyes.

"I'm a big fucking deal around here," he said, "You think the last cop beat you? Wait 'til Johnson Beal gets 'em out after you."

I grinned at him, slipped two crisp hundred-dollar bills from the wealth in his wallet and shoved them into my own pocket. I threw his wallet at him and it struck him in his face, spilling the rest of his money into the dirt.

"Go on and get the law," I said, "You can tell all about it on your radio show; how you were tempted by a boy and took him down a back road with your dick out."

He was stuffing money into his wallet, but he stopped and pointed a long, thin finger straight at my face.

"You think they'll believe that?" he said, "There ain't one person alive who's gonna take the word of a highway robber over the testimony of Johnson Beal."

"They might believe me when I tell about that tattoo of yours."

His righteous grin fell away from his face and he went deathly pale.

"It's just a small tattoo," I told him, "Still, it's bigger than that little dick you got."

I left him sobbing on the ground, took my pack from the backseat of his car and walked away into the woods. The breeze sighed in the trees and a raven cawed on the wing; the sounds of heaven and hell, still arguing over my life.

NINE
NO WELCOME HOME

I went deep into the woods, but the day was so still that I heard the low rumble of Johnson Beal starting his Cadillac and its tires crunching down the dusty road, back toward the highway. I was too exhausted to struggle with my tent, but I rolled out my blankets on a bed of leaves and lay my head against the earth.

My face was a hive of stinging wasps, my knuckles were swollen from beating Johnson Beal and I wasn't sure if the endless buzzing in my head was the echo of a concussion or the early noise of insanity.

I had been wrong about the road. I thought its mystery had been revealed when I let The Troll-Man go, but it hadn't been about him at all. He hadn't been an answer, just a question and a clue. I wasn't sure about the dreams and I couldn't call them visions, but I thought of an old woman I had known when I was a boy.

Her name had been Olga Jean and she was suspected of witchcraft, but she befriended me the summer my grandmother died and I came to love her dearly. She told me many things in the time I knew her; silly riddles, deep secrets and dark warnings, too, but the one thing I remembered most was something she said about me.

She told me once that I had dreamer's eyes, and every time I asked her what she had meant, she only told me to be careful in my dreams; and twice as careful *of* them after I woke up. As I grew older, I realized that the things I dreamed of lingered long into the day and I wondered if she had known, even then, that I was crazy.

I thought of the ghosts that had chased me through the southland; my mother and Elvis and even Huck, too, and I knew that I'd misunderstood their meaning. They had come at night as terrors, not to harm me, but to warn me off the road I'd been caught out on.

I called them ghosts, but in my heart, I knew the truth about their hauntings. The spell to raise the dead was one I learned when I was young and there's no magic to it, really; only memory and myth. No one dead comes back, unless we rob them from their grave.

I cried myself to sleep, weeping for my mother's ghost. From the day she died, I'd blamed her for the haunting of my heart, but maybe it was me who kept her ghost awake at night. Maybe it was me who robbed her of her resting peace.

In my dream, I was still a boy, ten years old and barefoot, running up a sidewalk after dark. It was the street that I grew up on, but something bad had happened, and the neighborhood was silent, all the streetlights dark and dim. A dust of dead locusts and daisies covered the ground, crunching between my toes and staining my heels, but I knew every ghost on the block and I wasn't afraid.

The neighborhood smelled like summer, but a dank and musky one, as if time had stood still for so long that it had finally started to rot. I saw my childhood friends, but none of them saw me, and all of them were grown; only I remained a child.

Our apartment door stood open, as if I were expected, and I rushed in brave and breathless to tell my mother I was home.

She wasn't there.

Everything in the apartment was dusted with the same foul fallout from the street and the record player turned, but there was no music, just a spooky popping crackle, like the devil gritting his teeth.

Down the hall, there was a light on in my grandmother's bedroom and I tiptoed to her door to see if she had died in peaceful sleep.

She died wide awake and she was looking at me.

I pushed open the door, peeked into the room and I found her on her bed, alive and waiting for me with the crinkliest of smiles. Her eyes were wet with tears and her arms were open for me, even after I had run away so long.

"I came home, Gramma!"

I leapt onto her bed and she wrapped her arms around me and she snuggled me against her like she always used to do.

"I came home," I said again, "Like Mom told me to do."

Gramma kissed my forehead and held me out to look at me, even though I hadn't changed one bit since the last time she had held me, nearly ten long years before.

"Richie's come home at last," she said, "But why? What would you come back here for?"

I stared at her a moment, blinked and shrugged my shoulders.

"So the bad man won't get me," I whispered, "Mom said I had to come back."

Gramma held me close again and stroked my hair, careful of the bumps and bruises that I got out on the road.

"Did she, Richie?" Gramma crooned, "Is that what your mother told you to do?"

I nodded and tears slipped from my eyes and I wondered why my mother wasn't there, why she hadn't been home and waiting up for me.

"Yes, Gramma," I said, "She told me it was time to go home."

Gramma sighed and shook her head.

"We're all dead here, honey. And even if it hurts, there's no welcome home left here for you."

I cried against her breast and she soothed me with the palm of her hand on the small of my back.

"But I ran all the way here..."

She lifted my chin to her long-lost smile and looked into my eyes.

Dreamer's eyes.

"But it's too late," she said, "Here, it's always late now, always late and always dark."

"But I don't know where to go," I sobbed, "No one knows me and nobody wants me. I'm just lost all of the time."

Gramma smiled.

"Maybe you're not lost at all," she said, "You always were a boy who followed his heart."

I glanced out the bedroom window. Night was falling on the street and gramma had fallen asleep. I turned to kiss her goodnight, but she wasn't sleeping and she wasn't snoring; she was rattling and she was dead.

I drew the sheets up over her face and left her bed, closed the apartment door behind me and chased the sunset down the block just as fast as I could run.

I woke up in the darkness and found my way out of the woods, back to the highway. I walked until the sun came up and just after dawn, I caught a ride into Lexington, Kentucky. I went downtown to the Greyhound station and bought a bus ticket with the money I had stolen from Johnson Beal.

TEN
GREYHOUNDS AND GHOSTS

I sat at the back of the bus, where smoking was allowed, and fell asleep against the window as the big Greyhound rumbled over the highway. I slept without dreaming and didn't wake up until we stopped at a small-town depot to take on riders. An old man shuffled slowly down the aisle and took the empty seat beside me.

"Mind if I sit here?"

I didn't mind and even if I did, he had bought a ticket to ride the bus, same as I had. He probably hadn't bought his ticket with blood money, either. I sat up in my seat and gave him room to settle into his own.

I couldn't get right back to sleep and I didn't feel like talking to the old man riding beside me. I smoked and stared out the window, watching the towns and the country roll by, with my headphones on and my Walkman tuned to an AM radio station.

I was low on batteries and the Walkman drained them fast playing cassette tapes, but I could listen to the radio the entire length of the eleven-hour bus trip. When we got nearer to a city, I would try to find a rock and roll station, but rolling over the countryside, all I heard were farm reports and news.

I had just about fallen back to sleep, with my head rocking gently against the seat, when the radio newsman startled me awake with a story out of Kentucky. A prisoner in the Eubank jail had set fire to a mattress and badly beaten the police officer who entered his cell to douse the flames. Officer Beaumont Dennison was recovering in a local hospital and the prisoner, William Axton Junior, had been sent back up the county with additional charges.

Axton had preached about God's dirty work, but ended up doing mine for the cost of a cup of coffee.

The old man tapped my shoulder and I took off my head phones and stared at him.

"You alright, kid?" he said, "You seemed to have had a start."

I shrugged.

"I just heard something on the news about someone I know."

"Oh," he said, "Not bad news, I hope."

I grinned.

"It could have been worse," I said, "No one got burned up alive."

He blinked at me and lit a cigarette. I had one, too, and we fell into talking.

We spoke for hours without any mention of the obvious, but he finally felt comfortable enough to ask me about the bruises and lumps on my face.

"If I'm tellin' you the truth," he said, "Your face looks about like a roadkill."

Roadkill.

"Sounds about right," I sighed, "I took a good beating yesterday morning."

He glanced at my hands.

"Them bruises and cuts on your knuckles tell me you give it back to him pretty good, yourself."

"I did that on another guy's face," I said, "Later in the evening, a little farther down the road."

He exhaled a mild curse, shook his head and wondered out loud how I managed to have two fights in one day.

"I just hit a bad stretch of road," I said, "Kept ending up in the wrong place at the wrong time."

The old man laughed and slapped my knee.

"Boy, there ain't any such thing as bein' in the wrong place," he said, "Ain't ever any wrong time for bein' there, either."

"How you figure that?" I asked him.

He sighed, took a long pull from his smoke and settled deeper into the seat.

"Son, every step you take upon this earth is known to God," he said, "He knows 'em even before you set one foot out on a road."

He blew smoke down the aisle of the bus.

"You may have bad times and end up in bad places," he said, "But that don't mean those times and places are the *wrong* ones. Everywhere you go, everything that happens to you; it's all God's way of putting you right where you're meant to be."

I argued with him and asked him why God would lead me down a road that only led to pain and darkness.

"Them bad places ain't anywhere God leads us," he said, "They're the places we end up in when we run away faithless and blind. You know the story of Jonah?"

I did. Jonah had been called by God to go to Nineveh and preach, but Jonah hid from God and tried to flee across the sea. His ship was caught in a great storm and Jonah was thrown into the sea and swallowed up by a great fish. He spent three days in the belly of the beast, but he prayed and God commanded the fish to spit him out.

"And where did Jonah go after that," the old man said.

"To Nineveh."

"That's right," he grinned, "And this may be a Greyhound bus you're ridin' on, but it might just be your fish, come to carry you away to where the Lord wants you to go."

I slept away the last two hundred miles of the trip and when I woke up at my stop, the old man had already gotten off the bus somewhere back along the road, most likely right where God had told him to go.

ELEVEN
EVERYTHING SOUTH OF HEAVEN

I claimed my duffel bag at the side of the bus, and took a taxi out of town and down the highway. It was a twenty-mile ride, but I had enough of Johnson Beal's money left in my pocket to splurge some on the fare. I saw familiar landmarks, a corner market and a laundromat, and told the driver where to let me out, He pulled off the road and grinned when I gave him a five-dollar tip on top of the fare.

He glanced out the window and his grin soured into a frown.

"You sure this is where you want me to let you out?" he said.

"Yeah, I'm sure. Why wouldn't I be sure?"

"It just ain't the best kind of neighborhood," he said, "But you got your business and I got my own."

I got out of the cab, hauled my pack out of the back seat and slung it over my shoulder. I walked across the highway and down a quiet street, where I met a gang of boys and young men standing out on a corner. I recognized some of their faces and some of them recognized me.

"Well, look who's back..." one of them said.

"What you doin' back around here?" another one said, stepping in front of me, blocking my way.

I sighed and let my duffel bag slump to the ground. Another boy stepped in close and two more came and stood just behind him.

"I'm not here for any trouble," I said, "I've had enough of it lately to last me."

The biggest boy, the one who had stepped in front of me first, looked over my swollen face and bruised knuckles.

"Looks to me like trouble's all you got," he said and the rest of the gang made threats and closed ranks around me.

There were too many to fight and I didn't want to stab any of them. I left my knife hidden under my shirt and made up my mind to take a beating, but a voice called out from the market, scolding the gang into silence.

"You all clear on off the corner and leave that half-white boy alone!"

Etta Simms came out of the market and crossed the street, leaning on a hand-carved cane and carrying a small sack of groceries. Some of the boys wandered off and the ones who had stayed were tamed by a stomp of her foot and a wave of the cane.

"You heard what I told you," she said, "This here boy is kin to Sneaks Thomas; his bastard son from New York City."

The boys stared at me in disbelief, but none of them argued against the wrath of Etta Simms.

"That's right," she said, "And you all know well and good they got family business to tend to at that house."

Family business?

Etta planted her cane firmly in the dirt, stood on her toes and stretched up to kiss my cheek. I blinked at her and she smiled at me sadly.

"You go on and see your daddy," she said, "Ain't none of these boys gonna bother you no more."

I took up my pack, left Etta Simms still scolding the neighborhood boys and crossed two ragged blocks to a porch where I had heard the blues and then confessed to them. I knocked on the door and heard faint footsteps, the soft sound of Converse high-top sneakers on a wooden floor.

For a moment, I was nervous about showing up unannounced, but I remembered what Miss Millie had told me the last time I'd been there.

You're as welcome here as you feel.

The door swung open and Sneaks stood on the threshold. He had been thin when I met him, but he seemed even thinner, almost gaunt. I had barely been away a week, but he had aged a year or more. His shoulders slumped and his face did, too, but then he recognized me and I was relieved that he hadn't lost his unbelievable smile.

"Bluesman..." he sighed, "Now, ain't this some kind o' surprise."

He stepped out onto the porch, pulled me into his wiry embrace and began to sob against my shoulder.

"Sneaks...what is it? What's happened?"

But I knew.

He stepped out of my arms, dragged his sleeve across his face and spoke out the meaning of heartache.

"My Millicent's gone," he whispered, "Gone away to heaven in her sleep."

"Oh, Sneaks," I moaned, "Oh, no."

He hung his head and every word he said was the sound of the blues.

"She passed the very next night after you was here," he sighed, "We laid her in the churchyard just yesterday 'noon."

Hot tears flooded my eyes and spilled down my swollen face.

"Will you take me to her?" I said.

At his son's church, Sneaks parked beneath a shady tree, leaned against the fender of the car and sent me to the cemetery alone.

"You go on and have your say," he told me, "I'll come along shortly."

He winked and I left him behind and followed a stone path to the rear of the church, where a mound of loose sod and a great trove of flowers hid the hole Miss Millie had gone through on her way to heaven.

She was buried beside the plot that held the bones of her son, Stanley Junior. I stood at the foot of her grave and silently sobbed and when I found my voice I said a prayer, though I was certain I'd forgotten how to.

"God..." I whispered, "I don't know You, but Miss Millie did, and I pray she's with You resting in tall comfort. Amen"

I knelt in the grass, placed my hand on the mound of earth and told Miss Millie why I'd come back to see her.

"You saved me," I whispered, "When God and the devil were shouting too loud and I didn't know what to do, I heard you. You were there."

A breeze passed over the headstones, a dog barked in the distance and the sun stood still right above me,

"I came back to tell you," I said, "But I got here too late. I'm always too late."

I felt a hand on my shoulder and rose from the grave to meet Sneaks' embrace.

"You ain't late, Bluesman," he said, "You come just when I needed you."

We sat on the porch, Sneaks with his guitar and me with my harmonica and he played a simple blues that I could follow. He had his cigar and I smoked cigarettes and I told him all that had happened since he dropped me off at the Mississippi, less than a week before.

I thought he might get angry when I told him how Roselyn had tricked me and robbed me of the money the church had given me, but he laughed for the first time all day and slapped his leg.

"Boy, that's about the most expensive hoo-ha kissin' lesson any fool ever had."

He shook his head and sighed when I told him how Dennison had beat me and left me stumbling bruised and blinded on the roadside.

"You was beat up the day I found you," he said, "And you come back lookin' ten times worse than *that*."

I told him all of my dreams, even the one that had fouled his son's church, how the Cadillac and the crows had stalked me all the way to Kentucky. He leaned forward on the edge of his chair when I named Johnson Beal and how I'd nearly killed him at the end of a dusty road.

"Miss Millie was right there with me, Sneaks. I swear, I heard her voice,"

He smiled at that and asked me what she said.

"She told me God hadn't given up on me yet," I whispered, "And that time, I believed her."

He leaned back in his chair and lit his cigar. He was quiet for a long moment, staring out across the dooryard at the moon.

"I'll tell you what, Bluesman," he sighed, "My Millie knew a thing or two about boys and she was right on the money 'bout you."

I grinned.

"Right about what?"

"She said you was gonna have to meet the devil face to face before you ever come to know that God is real."

"I saw him, Sneaks," I whispered, "I saw the devil face to face."

Sneaks strummed his guitar and stared at me through a lingering haze of cigar smoke and porch light.

"What about God?" he said, "Did you see his face, too, then?"

I sighed.

"I saw it," I confessed, "He's real, but I still don't trust him. He looks too much like the other one."

Sneaks threw his head back and laughed

"Well, Bluesman...that's a start."

He drove me a good, long way down the black snake highway, over the narrow bridge where I'd fought the Troll-man, past the all-night country store and the whispering trees to the county line. He pulled off the road and we sat in the car for a moment in silence.

"Where you gonna go?" he asked me.

I shook my head and stared through the windshield at the place where the highway shimmered up against the distance.

"I don't know," I said, "I don't think I'll know until I get there."

He reached in his pocket for his billfold, but I stopped him.

"I got money," I said, "I stole it from the preacher, but he stole it from God."

Sneaks laughed, but he took off his Ray-Bans and his eyes were misted over. We had sobbed throughout the day, but we both had tears left over and I cried with him once more before we parted.

"You got everything you need then?" he said, "To get on down the road."

"I got my harmonicas and my Springsteen tapes and a map I hardly look at," I said, "But I'll tell you something, Sneaks; I wish I had some pot and a pipe to smoke it."

He grinned from ear to ear and slapped my thigh and there was mischief in his eyes that even I was jealous of.

"What?" I said, "What's so funny?"

"Just you take a look inside that glove box," he giggled, "Just you have yourself a look-see."

I popped open the glove compartment and laughed until I nearly cried. There was a sandwich bag filled with dense green buds, a pipe fit for a wizard and two packs of rolling papers.

"Stanley Thomas!" I exclaimed.

"Strictly for my ailments," he sighed.

We sat together and passed his pipe until both of us were stoned and he gave me half his stash to ease me down the road. He wouldn't part with his pipe and I couldn't blame him, but he spared me a pack of papers and asked me if I knew how to roll a joint.

"I can roll a joint," I said.

"Well, you know what they say, Bluesman. Rollin' a joint is just about exactly like kissin' a woman's hoo-ha."

I slept that night beneath a clump of trees, thirty miles across the Oklahoma line. I dreamed of a road, somewhere on the flatlands, but there wasn't a cloud in the sky or a dust storm on the horizon. Huck was with me, too, bounding along at my side, with a clear blue sky above us and a long black highway below.

God was in His mansion, the devil slept under the earth and everything south of heaven was my home.

RADIO FREE HEAVEN

God's on the airwaves
Salvation, jubilation
Heaven's talking, talking
On the all-night station
No more angels on the highway
They're all dead from suicide
Holy bones paved in the blacktop
Of the roads on which we ride
  Hallelujah, hallelujah
  Jesus Christ was crucified
Satan's on the road again
He's come to claim the carcass
He's out walking, walking
Darker than the darkness
There's a devil on the highway
Just as sneaky as a troll
All the crows come for the murder
Of a boy without a soul
  Hallelujah, Hallelujah
  Loose the plagues, unseal the scroll
God's on the airwaves
He's just talk, talk, talking
But the devil's getting busy
And he's gone out walking

About the Author

Richard Holeman was born in New Jersey in 1966 and lives in southern California. In his youth, he spent years wandering the highways between Jersey and California, hitchhiking the interstates and back roads of America, trying to get lost, hoping to be found. His stories and poetry are inspired by his childhood and the neighborhood gang of kids he grew up with and by the years he spent living on the road. He is the author of First Boy on the Moon, Haloes are for Show-Offs and Never Ring a Witch's Doorbell.

39752914R00175

Made in the USA
San Bernardino, CA
21 June 2019